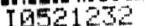

Other books by John Perrotta -

Racetracker "… a fascinating glimpse into a world unlike any other."

Amazon Reviews

"For a behind-the-scenes view of the eccentric and unpredictable world of horse racing, *Racetracker* is a sure bet."

Foreward Reviews

If Wishes Were Horses "… will grab you from the beginning and take you on a fascinating ride."

"… you can smell the turf, feel the heat in the shedrows, get track mud kicked in your face."

Amazon Reviews

Half a Chance "… steeped in the action and lore of the Thoroughbred race track … lots of fun."

Amazon Reviews

Out of Luck

"Best racetrack story since *Let It Ride*."

Amazon Reviews

At the End of the Bar
and other stories

By John Perrotta

First Edition.

Cover and illustrations by Jen Ferguson.

Short Dog Publishing

ISBN 978-0-578-83847-2

At the End of the Bar and other stories

By John Perrotta

Contents

VOODOO RIDER

Toby Neale stared at his boot, the side of it split where he had scraped the rail when his horse veered to avoid the spill ahead. White paint made a perfect horizontal line on the black patent leather and there were a few drops of blood on his white britches from the gash on his leg. His valet handed him a fresh pair of pants to wear for the next race.

"Close one," said Vasquez.

The valet had deep creases in his forehead and the nose he inherited from the Aztecs took over the rest of his face. The other jockeys called him Montezuma, but not usually when he could hear. The jockey and his valet were only a few years apart in age but hardly looked it. Neale had been nursing a moustache for years, trying to appear older, but his silky blonde hair made it a challenge.

"Too close," said Neale. "And it's getting damn tiresome."

"I had a time when I rode, about ten years ago, didn't win a race for six months," said Vasquez. "Sometimes it's just like that."

"This is different," Neale said. "Fourteen years, I've had my share of slumps, too. But never had to deal with this shit. I need a change, get myself away from here, and you know the reason why."

Vasquez sighed and inspected the damaged boot for possible repair.

"You mean again the mouse," he said.

"Fuck yeah that's what I mean," Neale said. "That Cubano sonofabitch left a dead rat right there."

He pointed his toe at the gap beneath his cubicle bench.

"I know it was him that did it," Neale said. "Last week there was a dead baby rabbit on the front steps of my house. And a bird on Friday morning and lizard with no tail on Saturday. Something every night. I know it's him 'cause he keeps giving me the stink-eye."

Vasquez scanned the room to see if anyone might be watching Neale's latest meltdown. A race was ready to start and several riders gathered at the television monitor over the desk where the Clerk of Scales sat making notes. Two others played cards on the top of a steamer trunk.

"C'mere," Vasquez said, holding a finger to his lips and motioning toward the room they used for their massage and physical therapy.

"I don't know if it's a Cajun curse, voodoo stuff, but Santeria priests, they call them, that kill chickens and pour the blood all over themselves," Vasquez said. "I think he's one of them, the Cuban. Maybe might have put one of those Santeria curses on you."

"He started it," said Neale. "Clipped my heels opening day and went down and came back to the room screaming at me like it was my fault. No-riding sonofabitch should be waiting tables someplace instead of getting in everybody's way out there. How the hell they give him a license, you tell me. Five days suspension he got. Should have been a month."

"I heard he was leaving, back to Florida," said Vasquez.

"Sooner the better," said Neale.

Vasquez wrote on the back of a mutuel ticket.

"Call this lady, Mama Dean, down the Quarter, she maybe can get the curse off you."

Neale took the slip of paper and looked askance.

"Sounds like bullshit to me," he said. "Voodoo bullshit."

"Okay. How many winners you ride at this meet?" asked Vasquez.

"Just the one, opening day," said Neale.

"And how many things like that happen?" Vasquez pointed at the gash on Neale's leg. "More than one?"

Neale nodded and said, "More than one."

"Plenty more. Two times you come off leaving the gate, and the one when the horse kicked you in the paddock, and this time you almost went over the rail. If it was me, that's what I'd do, go see Mama Dean. Get some herbs and stuff, get that curse off, amigo."

~~

Two weeks and a couple more close calls later, Neale was still aware of a jabbing pain in his groin if he moved the wrong way, and the chiropractor he'd seen a couple of times finally had his neck back to where he could turn his head all the way to his shoulder. He got beat on two favorites one day and drop-kicked his helmet into the grandstand and a couple of kids grabbed it and ran away.

He thought about the curse. All the time. Especially when he came home and found another bloodied carcass on his doorstep, mostly little birds, their skulls crushed, feathers strewn. He picked them up with a pair of tongs and placed them in a plastic grocery bag and mixed it in with the trash. The grisly encounters and the weight of his losing streak were rendering him antisocial, halfway a hermit. He never

4

answered the phone, and the girl he'd been seeing from the dentist's office finally stopped leaving messages.

When his agent hinted that maybe business would be better if he would come out in the morning and get on a few horses, Neale said it was time to make a change and he'd take care of his own business. So thank you and get lost.

"We're goin' for some etouffee, down to the little place off Hubbard Street," his valet said late one day. "Come on with us."

"I've had enough Cajun bullshit," Neale said. "Don't ask me again."

~~

Coming off the turn in front and into the stretch, Neale loosened the reins as his horse picked up speed. They opened up a length, then two, and when his mount changed leads he reached back to give him a slap with the whip to keep his mind on business.

He coughed. A handful of sand sprayed out of his mouth. The EMT was pouring water in his eyes to wash out some of the track dirt.

"Welcome back," said the EMT.

"How long? I was out?"

Neale was groggy, trying to focus.

"Long enough," said the EMT. "Good thing the track wasn't muddy, you might have drowned. I think you slid about twenty yards on your face. Remember anything?"

"I remember thinking I should get down flat, look good for the picture 'cause I was finally gonna win a fucking horse race."

"You were lucky you didn't get trampled," said the EMT. "Your horse jumped the rail after he propped and dumped you and ran around the infield for a while."

He put his case away and grabbed Neale's wrist to help him sit up.

"Thanks, Marco," said Neale.

"We have to stop meeting like this," said the EMT.

~~

The alley running between two restaurants was narrow and a sliver of light from the streetlamp lit his path on cobblestones that had been there since before the Civil War. Out on Bourbon Street a jazz quartet in one club competed with a blind blues singer in another, filling the thick night air.

Neale flipped up the collar of his jacket and tipped down the brim of his trilby, as if the couple exiting the door he was heading for might recognize him. He saw the girl looked like she had been crying, and neither one of them acknowledged his presence. He wondered why they would be visiting a place like this. He could say the same about himself.

The little cottage stood alone, peeling white paint with green roof shingles and shutters and Spanish moss hanging from the gutters. The black front door was slightly ajar, so he pushed it open without knocking and had to squint to see if anyone was in the room. The only light came from a couple of candles and the air was thick with the scent of a burning herb he didn't recognize, musky and not like the incense potheads use when they're trying to cover up the smell of reefer. Again he thought, what am I doing here?

Further inside he could only make out the woman's silhouette, a shape that resembled a mountain peak, filling the space at the other side of a small round table covered with an embroidered cloth.

"There, my friend," said the woman.

Her voice was raspy, smoky. She pointed to a three-legged stool across from her at the table. He took off his hat and did as she asked.

"Tell me why you come."

"It's about a curse," Neale said.

"A spell," she whispered.

"Yeah, something like that. I don't know. My mother raised me Catholic. They don't do those things."

She nodded, staring hard at him. He became conscious of his heartbeat, a little thump-thump-thump in his ears. His hands began to dampen.

"I'm a jockey, ride horses for a living. Over at Fair Grounds when it's open, Delta Downs and the Texas tracks when it's not."

He wondered if that was what she meant, or if he was supposed to tell her about growing up, taking a beating every day from his old man while his devout Catholic mother watched. Or living in a tack room in one of the barns at the racetrack before he was old enough to get a license, lying about his age and doing things he didn't want to do, just to stay alive.

"You are a good jockey?"

"I been leading rider a couple of times. It's what I do, I guess."

"More, tell me," she said.

He could see her better now that his vision had adjusted to the light, a round and coffee-brown face, her dark brown eyes almost black. No telling how old she was from an absence of lines or wrinkles, and she was smoking a skinny cheroot, flicking the ashes in a Mason jar. He couldn't see her hair, wrapped up in the red and yellow bandana like it was, and the huge gold earrings that dangled from her earlobes reminded him of little hubcaps.

"First day of the meet, I'm on a filly for Tee Red and this no-riding fool runs himself up my ass, clips heels and down he goes. Takes half the field with him and comes back to the jocks' room screaming it was my fault. Stewards suspended him for careless riding and next thing I know dead animals start showing up on my doorstep. First a rabbit, then two rats, then a mouse and a couple of canaries. I haven't won a race since then, but plenty other shit's happened to me. Vasquez – he's my valet – says it's maybe some kind of voodoo where they kill animals."

"Santeria," she said.

"Yeah, like that," he said.

"My valet says if he put a curse on me you could get rid of it," said Neale. "I don't believe in that stuff but it's been going on for a while and I'm trying anything."

"The man thinks you did him wrong."

"Yeah, the Cuban. He's gone now, left town, but I still can't win for losing."

"And it is the losing why you are here," she said.

Her words hung in the air. He felt his defenses wither and start to die.

"You don't know what it's like. They say there's a million ways to lose a race, and I feel like I'm running through them all. But that's the only way they keep score. You win or you're nothing. Less

9

than nothing. Doesn't matter if you're a fucking Mother Teresa on horseback, you don't win races who cares you were ever leading rider. You go back to the end of the line."

She was quiet for a moment.

"What you do, ride fast horses, you still have all your skills?"

"Hell yes I do," Neale replied. "Hell yes. But what happens when that ain't enough?"

"Put your hands on the table and close your eyes," she said. "And breathe through your mouth."

He felt her hands cover his. Hers were warm, small and pillowy, his were rough and boney, with bent, broken fingers. The room closed around them as she began a low moaning sound, which made him worry that she was going to make him chant, and if he did, would it work.

~~

Neale rubbed his eyes, slouched on the couch with the television tuned to some HBO rerun of a Will Smith movie with lots of things blowing up. He looked at his hands and rubbed the palms together, trying to recall the voodoo woman's touch. His fingers smelled like sage or lavender, he wasn't sure which.

There was a knock on the door and it opened before he could answer. His agent bounced in, full of positivity with a *Daily Racing Form* in his hand and parked himself in an easy chair. The chubby red-faced little man's given name was Sid but the racetrackers all called him Polly, half for his rosy attitude and half for the polyester suits he bought in the kids department at Macy's. Polly was smaller even than Neale and never dissuaded those who assumed he was a former jockey even though the closest he ever came to riding a horse was on the carousel in Asbury Park when he was a kid on the Jersey Shore. He still looked like a kid in some ways even though he was odds-on to have been born during the Eisenhower administration.

"How you feeling, Tiger?" said the agent. "Front page news. And they used your good side."

He displayed the cover of the *Form* like it was a trophy bass, plucked from the backwaters of the bayou. The headline article was about Neale and the breakneck pace he was setting. The accompanying photo showed him holding up four fingers signifying a four-winner day, atop a sweaty horse and surrounded by smiling owners. Neale studied the front page. The paper was yellowed, frayed at the edges.

"This is from last year," he said.

Polly grinned and shrugged.

"It was behind the box of hats I was keeping in my trunk. Thought you could use a reminder of how good you really are. Positive reinforcement, it's called."

"Didn't I fire you?" said Neale.

"Aw, you was just kidding," said Polly. "I wasn't around you wouldn't know where to get dinner. How'd it go with the witch doctor lady? I thought you'd be wearing a garlic necklace and beating a bongo. What did she do? Make you walk on hot coals? Drink frog's blood?"

"She said there was no curse, it's just a bad luck streak and that'll be forty bucks, sucker. She didn't say sucker but I know that's what she was thinking."

"So?" said Polly.

"When I got home I found out my neighbor next door's got a cat and that probably accounts for the rabbit and the canaries. And the mouse under my locker, he probably ate one of my diet pills and had a heart attack."

"Bravo!" said Polly. "Another curse lifted. Now go get some sleep. You breeze three tomorrow morning and ride six in the afternoon."

MY DOUBLEWIDE
NEIGHBORS

I shook out my trench coat and hung it on a peg on the wall. It was a Burberry I'd snagged for twenty bucks at a vintage clothing store back in L.A., marked down because of a cigarette burn on the sleeve. But it fit, and wearing it made me feel like Sam Spade. I watched a puddle gather on the floor.

"Does it ever do anything but rain here?" I said, neither expecting nor getting an answer.

Gwen was sitting in a straight-backed chair, the one she'd stripped of its chipped white paint, with a view out the trailer's dirty bay window at the tumble-down mobile home across the rutted, muddy road that passed for a street.

"Nobody has left that place in days," Gwen said reaching for a battered paperback.

"They hunker down in there like hibernating bears," I said.

"I hope those kids are okay."

"They can't be home-schooling," I said. "He'd have trouble spelling his own name with a head start, and she couldn't count without using her fingers."

"I haven't seen any kids in a while," Gwen said, losing interest. "Maybe they belong to somebody else, just visiting. Or grandkids or something."

"And there's lights on all hours of the night," I said. "Any chance they're just insomniacs?"

"Maybe you should go check," she said, flipping open her book. "No, don't."

Across the road, the rainwater was running off the roof of the neighbor's doublewide onto a pile of junk, mostly tires and auto parts liberated from the collection of ancient Dodge Darts rusting away in the trailer park side yard.

"We should go home," she said. "Go back where we belong and be broke. It's not worth it living here just for the exchange rate. I'm sick of tortillas and beans. I'd kill for a loaf of Italian bread."

"It's not so bad," I said.

Her eyes got dreamy.

"A fresh ciabatta," she said. "Dip it in olive oil and balsamic vinegar with a little salt and pepper."

"So I'll score you some bread," I said. "At least here we don't owe anything to anyone."

~~

14

We had left L.A. six months earlier in debt to our eyeballs with less than two thousand bucks to show for my half-a-dozen years busting my ass with start-ups in the tech world. Somebody was winning big in that game, but it sure wasn't me.

Gwen's patience had grown thin, hardly a surprise. She was getting sick of the old leches patting her backside in the cocktail lounge where she waited tables five nights a week so we could afford our one-bedroom rental in Tarzana.

Time for a change, we decided. Either that or split up. I was genuinely surprised she had hung in with me for so long, what with the losing streak on the ponies at Santa Anita that had been shrinking my paycheck on top of everything else. It was hard to tell if we were staying together for love or just out of habit. The word divorce had entered more than one heated conversation. But those can be expensive, too, so we weighed our options and decided to go with a change of scenery.

Costa Rica sounded attractive, but by the time we paid for plane fares we'd be starting at the bottom there with little chance of making any money, at least doing anything legal. Instead, we spread out a map of Mexico on the kitchenette table, figured how far three days of steady driving south could take us, and drew a circle around the Gulf Coast town of Tampico.

~~

The Volvo's four cylinders sipped gas across California, Arizona, New Mexico and a chunk of Texas, at which point we took a hard right at San Antonio and finished the last leg of the trip in a 12-hour haul, straggling past a scattering of oil rigs on the outskirts of Tampico just before dark.

It wasn't long before we started to think we might be on to something good. Food was cheap, Tecate was a buck a bottle, and a fresh January breeze blew off the Gulf of Mexico. For temporary digs we pre-paid the weekend at a motel that would have earned zero stars in a travel guide but made up for its seediness with what we decided to call "ambiance." The next morning, I found a real estate agent who spoke just enough English to find us a doublewide we could rent in the Vista del Mar trailer park near the coast. The "view" was of the "ocean" if you stood on the roof, but the price was right at a hundred twenty-five a month.

It was our little slice of low-rent paradise for at least a couple of months until the humidity returned in all its unforgiving glory. Seems our arrival had coincided with the coolest winter they'd had in years, one of those La Niñas that turned the weather upside down, and when atmospheric order was restored the damp air poured over us with a vengeance, like a rogue wave rushing a dry beach.

But at least we were getting along, which was, for a change, pretty damn nice.

~~

It was an hour maybe at most since the tide had turned, seawater pouring out of the estuary, fleeing as if it were frantic to escape. From where I stood on the shore, I could see the beach on the other side, with at least three hundred yards of fast-moving water in between. In a few hours the whole inlet would be nearly dry, like a drained bathtub.

"More oysters, *senor*?" he said.

The old man had dirty sleeves rolled past his elbows, his face the color of a tobacco leaf etched with a hundred lines from a relentless Mayan sun doubled in intensity by its reflection off the glassy waters of the Gulf.

"*No, gracias*," I said, shaking my head and sprinkling some Tabasco on the last of my serving of salty bivalves before sucking it off its gnarled shell.

He nodded and moved on, slipping out of his huaraches before taking a dozen sinking steps over the muddy shore, shepherding a pair of the floating plastic trays repurposed to hold his catch.

He washed the oysters a few times, shifting them from crate to crate to rinse off the silt before

17

submerging the plastic bins again in the brine while using a piece of clothesline to secure them to a wooden stake.

"You need oysters, you see me," he said, climbing back onto dry land. "Anything else, *senor*, you tell him."

The old man nodded toward a husky figure in black twenty or so yards up the beach who appeared to be menacingly teasing a young woman standing knee deep in the shallows.

"I'm good," I said, figuring that "anything" from a guy dressed in black in these parts could mean anything from a bag of weed to a load of smack or a dark-haired teenage girl.

I turned back to the old man, who was well on his way to what was probably his home, in this case a gutted trailer with only three walls.

"*Viejo!*" I called out, waving.

He shuffled back.

"Here," I said and slipped him a five-dollar bill, well beyond the local standard for even an extravagant tip. "*Por usted.*"

I was pushing my Spanish near its limit.

"*Muchas gracias, amigo*," he said. "Thank you."

I turned and he was gone, but I knew giving up a five-spot for nothing in particular would probably save me plenty in the long run. By contrast, I also knew if I asked the man in black for anything, he'd consider that he owned me. He'd be there every time I turned around - in the village, at the taco stand downtown, here on the beach. He'd consider me part of his clientele, and not in a friendly way. I wanted to be just a gringo customer of the old man, an unimportant stranger. Maybe then the man in black would leave me alone.

~~

I detoured through the farmers' market on the way home, intending to buy as much of the local produce as I could carry, along with a jar of the fiery green salsa for which Gwen had developed an addiction. It was a weekday and not as busy as usual, so when someone tapped my elbow I expected it to be just another random hustler trying to fob off some cheap jewelry or steer me to the cubicle where his brother or his uncle or his cousin sold fish, "caught fresh this morning."

This hustler produced his best smile, the one they all used to disarm hapless tourists. There was a stain on the front of his dark shirt, a remnant of yesterday's lunch, and he needed a shave.

"No oysters here," said the man in black.

"S'cuse me?"

"You're the *amigo* of Felix," he said. "I see you there for the oysters."

I avoided eye contact and gathered my packages, nodded and made ready to split, at which point he flashed a badge – a little one, gold, in a leather wallet.

"*Narco*," he said.

"Oh yeah, *si*, right."

"We have to talk," he said.

"No drugs for me," I said. "Just some whisky once in a while or a beer."

"I know," he said. "We been watching you since you come here."

This was not comforting in the least. He told me he was in charge of busting up a drug smuggling ring and I was going to help him. It was not a request. I was going to be a beard in a drug buy and he gave me directions to a bar where I should wait for someone to give me something. He didn't say what the something was, but I could guess. Hearing it said out loud wouldn't have made me feel any better.

~~

Like all watering holes in that part of town, the *taberna* I was sent to had only minimal lighting and a décor that could only be described as shabby chic, but without the chic. No windowpanes, just wooden shutters, and metal chairs and tables that might have been castoffs from some dreary government office.

I took a seat at the end of the deserted bar and waited, while doing precisely what I'd been told to do, which was read my week-old American news-paper and order a beer.

The lumbering bartender shoved a bottle of Tecate my way and rubbed fat fingers on the bloated belly beneath his stained t-shirt. I tossed a few *pesos* his way and nursed the beer as long as I could before calling for another. An hour went by, considerably more than the ten minutes I was led to expect, but local time was languid, and who was I to rush the wheels of justice.

My second beer was tepid, almost warm by the time a pair of *gringos* arrived and parked themselves on the barstools to my left. The blonde next to me wore her wavy hair loose, cascading halfway down her back.

"Hi ya," she said with a toothy smile, extending her hand. "I'm Jennifer."

I tried hard but failed to keep my eyes off her enormous rack straining the limits of her tank top.

"P-Parker," I said, finally remembering my name.

"He's Bones," she said, nodding towards the skinny guy to her left. I gave Bones a weak wave and stared at him a moment too long before going back to Jennifer's tits. I'd heard the expression "pencil neck" before, but I'd never seen one in the flesh, until now.

"Parker," I repeated as if he might not have heard.

The three of us did the "where ya from?" routine and all agreed that being warm and dry in God-forsaken Tampico, ugly as it was, was a damn sight better this time of year than freezing Boston or crowded L.A. And eminently more affordable, as Bones noted when their beers came.

"She don't really like it that much here," he said. "Always finds something to rag about."

"It's not that I don't like it," Jennifer said, deploying a pout. "It's just that I get them hot flashes."

"I don't know how I'm going to be able to stand the summer," I said. "My wife and I got here in November, and it was okay for the first couple of months. But I never knew it could get so humid you could sweat through your socks."

"You got an old lady?" said Bones. He draped his arm over Jennifer's shoulder and played with her ear, flicking at her dolphin-shaped earring.

"My wife's an artist," I said. "Wood carvings. We came for some peace and quiet and to make a new start. But I think she's already gotten over the solitude."

I was running dry on small talk, and if this scruffy twosome was my drug buy contact, they were taking their sweet time getting to the point.

"Gotta watch out for these hustlers," Bones said, glancing over his shoulder. We were the only ones in the bar.

"Gwen and I kind of keep to ourselves," I said.

"Gwen being your unhappy wife?" Jennifer said. "So, what do you do?"

"I used to work with computers, but I thought I'd come here and take a break. Wait 'till I think of something else. Maybe write some poetry."

"Poetry," she said, nodding. I might as well have said "physics."

"Computers," Bones said, nodding along. I clearly had them stumped.

"I was what they called a code monkey," I said, summoning the derogatory term favored by self-superior techies. "I have to admit, I just did it to make a living. I didn't really like staring at a screen all the time."

"I don't do computers," she said. "I think the government watches you. Trying to catch you nekked."

Bones nodded agreement.

"Better down here," he said. "They can't afford all that electronic crap. Here, you can do whatever you want."

He lifted his beer in a toast to the spirit of a Mexican ideal I hadn't yet come to appreciate.

"We're in import-export," Jennifer went on. "Pottery, mostly. If you need any, you can have it wholesale, being you're one of us."

I looked at my watch. I'd been sitting there for two hours and twenty minutes that I'd never get back. I downed the last of the latest and warmest Tecate and scooped most of my change off the bar.

"Well, nice meeting you," I said.

"You too," she said, giving her teeth an encore.

"See you around, homey," he said.

~~

I was stiff from sitting. I stretched, shaded my eyes from the midday sun and slid behind the wheel of the Volvo. As I went to turn the key, the hand that touched my right shoulder had the same effect on me as a switch being thrown on the electric chair.

"Goddamn," I blurted and looked in the mirror to see my narco friend staring back from the rear seat. I might have peed a bit.

"I waited over two hours, but nobody came," I said.

24

He made a sound somewhere between a snort and a cough. It was not reassuring.

"This suitcase," he said, patting a fake alligator valise on the seat next to him, "you give to your friends at the trailer park."

There was a paper tag with an address attached and a small lock.

"Friends?" I said. "What friends?"

"Across your street," he said.

"You mean those neighbors in the beat-up green doublewide? The ones we never see?"

"Yeah, them."

"They're not my friends," I said. "We … we barely know them. Might have talked to the guy twice since we're here. I think his name is Aubrey, but I don't even know his wife's name – Beverly or Bernadette or something starts with a B."

He leaned close to my ear. His breath was at least fifty proof.

"I doan give a fuck if you go over and sleep between the two of them and let them stroke your lily-white ass," he said.

"Lily" sounded like lee-lee and for some reason that amused me. I smiled. It might have been the two hours of warm beer.

"You think this is funny, *gringo* motherfucker?" he said. "My boss might be just as happy, I arrest your pussy-ass and throw you in a cell with some real bad boys, maybe guys who roll you over and give you a ride. You like that, maybe?"

"No," I said. "No, no. I'm just pointing that out, that those people are not our friends."

"You take this over, knock on the door, and give it to him. You say, 'Paco sent me.' He will give you a bag and you take it from him. Then walk away. You got it? 'Paco sent me.'"

"Can I ask a question?"

"Go ahead."

"What's in the suitcase?"

"Ask something else."

"Is this dangerous?"

"Hah!" he laughed. "Not unless you screw it up. Then we might have to shoot you. And whatever you do, doan open it. You would not like what happens."

With that he slapped the back of my head, popped open the back door, and disappeared into the jungle growth behind the bar. I sat frozen, hyperventilating with my hands squeezing the steering wheel in a white-knuckled death grip. I wracked my brain for choices but came up with nothing that didn't end in some flavor of grief. I stumbled out of the car, gasping for breath, and made a beeline into the *taberna*, where I slammed a shot of rye and drained a beer just to get my heart to stop bouncing off my ribs.

Jennifer and Bones were long gone. It was just the bartender, who didn't bother to make eye contact as he demanded payment for the drinks. I abandoned the change and headed for the door, determined somehow to bring an end to what had become a living nightmare. I was only a couple of steps outside when I pulled up short and let out a low moan.

The Volvo's rear passenger side door was wide open, and the fake alligator suitcase was gone.

~~

I don't remember driving back to Vista del Mar, but when I walked in our trailer, Gwen was drying her hair. It was long and auburn, and she usually wore it in pigtails. I asked her to stop while I told her about my conversation at the market and the narco in my back seat and what he told me to do with the suitcase.

"Can't you call him and tell him you got robbed?" she said from the bathroom.

"We didn't exactly exchange personal information," I said. "It wasn't like an optional deal, as if I had any chance to decline. He said 'they' were watching me. They've been watching us. For how long I don't know, maybe since we got here."

"And they think that fat putz across the way is a gangster?" she said. "That Aubrey?"

"I don't know what they think," I said. "Or why they picked me for whatever the fuck is going down. I just want to disappear."

I was at the bureau, taking my socks out of the drawer, refolding them and putting them back. I did this three or four times before starting on my boxers. Gwen was back at the kitchen table, opening her laptop.

"Let's see if we can make some sense of this," she said, calling up her search engine. "I'll look for 'Tampico drug busts.'"

This was typical Gwen, trying to tamp down my hysteria with cold logic and sensible answers. I stopped folding my underwear and went along with it as she found thirty-six references. She clicked on a promising link and up came a photo of a short, stocky man with a three-day beard, identified as Oliver Barnett of no fixed address.

"I guess he could be Aubrey," I said over the increased buzzing sound in my ears. "Not that it makes me feel any better."

"What are you going to do?" she asked.

I was about to answer, *I have no fucking idea,* when we were drawn to the sound of a car coming to a sliding stop in front of the trailer across the road.

We looked out our bay window to see Jennifer and Bones emerge from a beat-up Toyota 4Runner and head for the neighbor's door. Bones was carrying a suitcase – *the* suitcase, taken from my car. Neighbor Aubrey, wearing cargo shorts and a ratty Hawaiian shirt, opened the door and gave Bones a high five before ushering them inside.

"So those lowlifes are doing your job?" Gwen wondered aloud. "Maybe you're off the hook."

"I should be so lucky," I said.

After a few minutes, Jennifer and Bones alighted from the trailer carrying a dark green duffel bag that appeared to be stuffed to its limits.

"What the hell is going on?" said Gwen. "I'm having trouble figuring who's the cops and who's the robbers."

The Toyota peeled out, spraying mud in its haste. An eerie silence descended upon the neighborhood, disturbed only by the sound of a macaw kept by an old woman who lived two spaces down. Then, without warning, we were thrown to the floor as the front windows shattered with the force of an explosion that blew apart the trailer across the street in a towering fireball. I jumped to cover Gwen as heat from the explosion surged through our broken windows.

"Holy fuck," she said.

"Holy fuck," I said.

When we finally summoned the courage to have a peek, about the only thing recognizable in the trailer space across the street was a few of the cinder blocks on which our neighbor's doublewide had been mounted. A lonely, smoldering Barcalounger sat the middle of what remained of their living room floor.

In my shocked state of mind, for some reason I thought, *Well, at least now we have an unobstructed view of the oil tankers floating in Tampico Bay.* I checked our carport to find the back tires of the Volvo rendered flat as tortillas. Its rear window had imploded, and the paint had blistered, leaving the car looking like a pale-yellow toad.

More troubling, though, was the black SUV with heavily tinted windows that had pulled up behind the car and the sight of my narco friend striding toward our front door.

"Here he comes," I said.

She was already in the bedroom.

"We're packing," said Gwen.

Even so, it was no use trying to pretend we weren't home. Once inside, he looked around the trailer with disdain, curling his lip at the New York Yankees banner on the wall over my prized Louisville Slugger, signed by Derek Jeter himself.

"*Yanquis,* uh," he spat. "Where's my money?"

I explained what had transpired at the bar, describing the two thieves, and the subsequent inferno that had erupted across the street in the wake of their exchange with my neighbor. My late neighbor. He was silent, walking around the room. He went in the kitchen, opened the fridge, and grabbed a can of beer. After sucking most of it down in one long gulp, he produced an enormous handgun and placed it on the coffee table, then slumped onto the couch.

"I know she's in there," he said, nodding toward the bedroom's closed door. "Tell her to get her ass out here."

Beyond Gwen in the doorway, I could see our two suitcases on the bed, both open and half filled. She stood a few feet from me as he picked up the gun, moved closer, and stuck it in my face.

"I tole you not to screw it up," he said.

He took a step back and turned his attention to Gwen, pointing his gun first in her face and then slowly lowering it the length of her torso. He spoke to me.

"Before I kill you, maybe first some fun," he said.

Outside, what was left of the neighbor's flaming trailer crackled and popped. The buzzing in my ears was deafening. Gwen leaned back, covering her face, offering just enough of a distraction for me to grab

Jeter's bat from its rack on the wall and take a swing at his head. I missed my target, but when he raised his hand to block, I hit the pistol. It fired a wild shot that ricocheted off the wrought iron light fixture hanging from the kitchen ceiling. The bullet, still possessed of sufficient velocity, hit him squarely on the top of the head. He looked startled, then dropped to the floor.

"Is he dead?" Gwen said.

It was hard to tell whose eyes were wider. I felt his neck for a pulse and found none.

"Oh boy," I said.

Across the street, half a dozen firemen in yellow slickers and helmets had arrived and were hosing down the cinder blocks and the Barcalounger. An ambulance pulled away, likely containing what was left of our neighbors. One of the firemen was crossing the street, heading for our front door.

"Here, come on," I said, grabbing one of the dead man's arms while Gwen grabbed the other. We slid him into the bedroom, leaving a trail of crimson on the tan shag rug.

"Tell him we're okay," I said, and she went to answer the knock at the door.

~~

"I told him we were fine," Gwen said a few minutes later. "That maybe they could come back tomorrow to check on us. I didn't understand a word he said, but maybe my '*muy bien*' and '*mañana*' took care of it."

We watched as the firetruck headed back toward town while we sat on the couch next to each other, trying to make sense of what had just happened. There was also the dead guy in the bedroom. Gwen brought the suitcases out and put them on the couch. She started packing again, essentials only. The Jeter bat and the banner went in my bag, the seashells from the coffee table in hers.

"We should just leave," she said. "Before the police get here."

I stepped over the stiff to get my boxers and my socks, my t-shirt collection, and my jeans. The rest could stay.

"We should take his car, get to the station, and get on a bus to Laredo before anybody comes looking," she said.

"I guess telling the police what happened probably wouldn't work," I said.

"That might be hoping for a lot," she said. "Pretty complicated conversation. With your grasp of the language, I mean. And who would believe it?"

I felt a wave of despair roll over me. I sat on the edge of the bed and looked at the body and for some reason began to cry.

"You go," I choked out. "Save yourself."

She moved next to me and put her arms around my neck, kissed me on the cheek and rubbed my back until I stopped sobbing.

"Okay," she said. "I'll tell your father what happened. Maybe he knows somebody who knows somebody down here."

And that was that. She picked up her suitcase and headed for the front door.

"Sorry it didn't work out," she said.

I shivered, and I was still staring at the door when I heard her gun the SUV's engine in what was, without question, a goodbye.

~~

The thing about Mexican jails, at least those found in the smaller towns, is that they all aspire to the same standards, which are basically none.

The tank here in Tampico is considered especially nice, according to my incarcerated brethren, but I've been in condemned buildings ready for demolition that were five-star Marriotts compared to this.

The story that followed me here, embellished somewhat, was that I had been caught in the middle of a shoot-out with some rogue cops involved in a drug scam, and that I had dispatched the one who was particularly disliked by the locals for his

34

shakedowns. When I gave the authorities the bent narco, with only his fingerprints on the gun and my version of the ricochet, they had to hold me until they could figure it all out. In the meantime, I had what could be considered hero status in the cellblock for avenging several of my fellow inmates.

I haven't heard from Gwen, but I know she contacted my father. With any luck and only a couple of payoffs, according to the lawyer he hired, I could be out of here in a few days. Then I'll be on my way back to the code monkey jungle, where the only threats come from bad posture and poor lighting. I might even give the ponies at Santa Anita another chance.

JOE'S TURN

Turner topped off his cup from a coffee pot that had been simmering there on the back burner for the past three hours. He needed a shower and his greying hair was beginning to creep over the back of his collar. *The Treasure of the Sierra Madre* was on the TV, and with the bags he had under his eyes and his three-day beard he could have been one of the miners. Lilly held up a hand, waving him off from her cup.

"Coffee at nine o'clock?" she said. "Probably not a good idea."

He stared into the coffee cup, then watched as she pulled her hair back in a ponytail and began clearing the kitchen table. Around her neck she still wore the gold horseshoe with a small diamond that he gave her twenty years ago on their first anniversary.

"Probably should have another beer instead."

"Probably neither one, for someone who hasn't been sleeping."

Him wondering why he felt like the time in the hospital, the last time he rode, when his horse clipped heels and down they went. Remembering they told him he'd been nicked by another horse's shoe, right behind his ear and was lucky he didn't get his skull cracked. And the way she sat there by his bed for how many nights until he awoke and she was there crying, just glad he was still alive.

"The feed man cut me off today. I had to borrow two bags of oats from Todd but he isn't in great shape himself. And the tack man came by at break time and took back the two bridles and saddles I got last month."

She put her hand on his.

"I'm sorry, Joe."

"Hard to train horses without saddles."

"Or hay and oats. So?"

"So, listen, I've been wanting to tell you, but..."

She thought she saw a glimmer of a tear in the corner of his eye.

"You're leaving me for one of the exercise girls."

He laughed and wiped his nose on the back of his hand.

"Nah, worse. I did something stupid. Moscowitz told me he could either pay me the fifteen thousand he owes on his training bills out of what's in the purse account or claim another horse for him. But he couldn't do both."

"And of course, you claimed the horse."

"For sixteen, and he made me put up the other thousand."

"Where'd you get the thousand?"

He slipped back into an old habit and gnawed on his thumbnail.

"Part of the ten grand his cousin Pinky loaned me. All my help have been waiting three weeks without getting paid, so I had to do something or I'd be mucking out fifteen stalls myself."

"A guy called Mouse Moskowitz has a loanshark cousin named Pinky? Why didn't he lend *him* the money? What kind of people are we dealing with, the twenty percent bloodsucking kind? Jesus."

"I didn't have any choice, had to pay the grooms."

She shuffled a stack of dunning letters.

"And how many owners *don't* owe us on their bills?"

"The two guys that own the grey mare are paid up."

"And we haven't won a race since Memorial Day," she said. "Maybe I should take the kids and go to my mother's. So's they don't have to be here to watch when the gangsters come to break your legs."

He poured the rest of coffee in the sink.

"I'm going to Marty Beller's office tomorrow and put my foot down. He's another one who has been stringing me for too long. If he stiffs me you can call your brother and tell him I'll take that job on the landscape crew. If he'll still have me."

~~

Joe Turner parked his pickup truck in a guest spot in the nearly empty parking lot. It was a Ford 150 he inherited when his father passed away three years ago and he never bothered to get the cracked windshield or the bashed fender on the passenger side fixed. He had been practicing his lines on the way over, remembering how he always seemed to get the short end of the conversation when he went to see this guy, the one he thought of as a fat pig, but a fat pig with a lot of money. For the four years he trained for Beller, never once had he gotten paid on time, except the odd occasion when they won a race and the track would pay him his ten percent directly. But he always had to chase the guy for his training fees. Lilly said the man was treating Joe like he was a credit card, only he didn't even pay the interest.

Joe sunk in the leather armchair, across from the ruddy face looking down on him from the other side of a glass-topped mahogany desk. He figured the chair he was sitting in was that soft and low so you'd sink into it and be captive, unable to move. The guy's mane of white hair reminded him of the mullet sported by one of the Panamanian exercise boys.

The mullet told Joe the six horses he had in training had cost him over three hundred fifty thousand, but he wasn't throwing another cent of good money after bad, no sir. Not even for the Bernardini colt he had named Papa Chico after his father, the one that had cost two-hundred-thirty grand. He slid a stack of registration papers and a bill of sale across the desk.

"All yours, buddy," he said. "The whole bunch. Now we're even."

Joe tried to tell him he didn't need a bunch of horses to feed, he needed the fifty thousand for the back training bills so he could pay his help and the feed man and the tack man and the van man, but the mullet just said adios pal, take that or take nothing. Or sue me but don't let the door hit you in the ass on the way out.

~~

"What are we supposed to do with these?" asked Lilly as she sorted through the pile of foal certificates.

"The Bennett brothers will take the four geldings for their feed bill and try to make polo ponies out of them," said Joe. "And Todd said he'd give me five thou' for the filly for a broodmare. At least I can get the saddles back."

She scrutinized one of the foal papers, holding it up to the light hanging over the table.

"Looks like a stock certificate. Wasn't this Papa Chico one the yearling he bought at that auction in Kentucky? For a lot? The time when you thought that bloodstock agent screwed him?"

Joe nodded. "Except now it's dead lame," he said. "Got a chip in his ankle that the vet says probably can't be operated on. Just enough to keep him from running but not enough to keep him from eating. I put a working blister on it so maybe he gets sound enough that we can sell him for something. Took me six months to talk Beller into running him for a tag and the day I entered him he came up with the chip. The chip that broke the camel's back.

"That's when he told me he wanted to sell everything and I told him they weren't worth what he owed, stupid me. Should have lied to him and got paid."

"I know what most guys do," she said. "They look out for themselves first. You spend all your time trying to save pennies for millionaires and what do they do but screw you. My father told me when the ship is sinking, it's every rat for himself. What about the guys you play poker with? Maybe sell it to one of them. They're always wanting to bet on them, maybe it's time they own one. Or sell some shares. I saw a movie where they did that with a play on Broadway."

"For a horse that might never run?"

"Bunch of dummies want to give you money, you should take it. My brother says he just laid off two guys but you can mow grass part-time if you want. Personally, I'd take those guys for all they have and pay some credit card bills. In the movie they thought the play was a stinker and it turned out to be a hit. Pretty funny."

"So much for the Golden Rule, eh?"

"Daddy said the one who has the gold makes the rules and you should do it to them before they do it to you."

"Pretty strong words for a preacher."

"He only did that on Sunday. Rest of the time he sold insurance."

~~

For the next three weeks, on every Saturday morning, one of Joe's poker buddies would show up at the barn. He came with his kids and brought carrots to feed to the big chestnut colt with the flaxen mane and tail. And Joe's mechanic showed up around the same time, on his way to the shop.

Joe showed them how to break the carrots into small pieces and offer them to the horses.

"Hold your hand flat, like this," he told them, and they laughed and squealed when the colt stuck out his tongue for them to tug on. Joe had the littler kids stand on an overturned feed tub to have their picture taken.

On Sunday mornings Joe's barber would come to the barn and sit in the chair outside his office. He was a single man on his own, said he had nowhere particular to go and just liked to watch the horses walk while he drank his Starbucks. Joe's eye doctor came with his wife too and a little later in the morning his dentist would drop by with his mother on their way home from church.

Joe liked the way their eyes would light up when he said, "Come on, let's watch your horse."

Reginald White, one of the poker players who worked at the bank, came the morning after their Thursday night game and gave Joe fifteen thousand in banded hundreds to hold his two shares. He said he'd bring the other forty thousand by the end of the week and Lilly said she'd never seen that much money in cash. Reginald said he was going to surprise his wife, that she always wanted to own a horse, so he wanted to keep it their little secret. Lilly thought Reginald was pretty pompous, with the gold watch fob he wore with his three-piece pinstriped suit and his affected manner of speech, the way he tried to speak like Cary Grant, but she told Joe the money was good and cash never bounced like some of the checks the mullet gave them.

None of the new partners dickered on the price after Joe showed them the *Blood-Horse* magazine article about the colt that had sold for so much money in Kentucky, they just anteed up for their twelve and a half percent or their six and a quarter percent or their three percent. They were all so excited to be horse owners that none ever asked for any paperwork.

Joe told Lilly it was funny how most of them couldn't tell one horse from another, even the chestnuts from the bays.

By the time Papa Chico had a dozen new owners, Joe had a new Ford 150 and Lilly had a new Lexus SUV. Lilly paid the kids' tuition and all their credit card bills out of a company she formed from an online service and christened Phoenix Stable, since the way she saw it, they were coming back from the ashes.

Joe kept a big jar full of red and white peppermints on his desk for everyone to feed the horses. He figured out that the peppermints were a good investment, considering each one of the new partners were paying him from twelve to twenty dollars a day times thirty days, which came to over five grand a month for just the one horse. Joe couldn't understand why he hadn't thought of it sooner.

~~

They were at the kitchen table finishing a couple of New York strips Joe had burned on the grill, potatoes wrapped in aluminum foil and some asparagus from Lilly's garden. He poured her another glass of the nice California Pinot they had taken a liking to.

"Had a strange dream last night," said Joe.

"You and the two blondes again?" said Lilly.

"Very funny."

"At least you slept. Usually, you wake me up when you can't and then I can't get back to sleep myself."

"Dreamed I was climbing these wooden stairs full of holes that wrapped around the side of a wall like a spiral staircase. I felt like I might fall through the holes. And the stairs kept getting smaller and narrower until they got to nothing. And they were tilted, on an angle. Very disturbing. And there was a dog, a huge black and white pit, right in the middle of it. Wouldn't let me by, kept snarling like he wanted to tear me to pieces."

"And how did it end?"

"Me waking up, what else?"

~~

46

The winner's circle looked like a three-ring circus. The track photographer had to hand off his camera to an assistant while he tried to herd nine men, seven women and five of their kids out of harms way as Joe Turner grabbed the reins of his wound-up colt, spinning and kicking out.

"Twenty-four copies for you, Joe?" asked the photographer as he took the shot.

Turner gave him a thumbs-up.

"Maybe make it twenty-eight."

"You got more owners than IBM."

Joe laughed and ushered his herd out the gate.

"Mister Turner?" asked one of the women.

"Ma'am?" said Joe.

"Would it be possible if we came back to the barn and gave him some carrots? I mean, treat him for winning? And the kids could get some pictures for show and tell."

"Absolutely," said Joe. "But first he goes to the test barn because he won. He should be home in his stall in about half an hour."

"Thank you so much," she said and went to gathering her brood.

~~

Lilly brought their dinner out to the table on the back porch. The frogs and crickets were chirping in the field next door and fireflies dotted the back yard. She raised her wine glass.

"To Papa."

"To Papa and all his owners," said Joe, returning the toast.

"You don't want them to compare notes," said Lilly.

"No chance," said Joe. "They all keep apologizing to me when they ask questions. They think since they only own a small piece they're not entitled to speak up. They're too busy anyway, getting their licenses and their passes and I made sure Amy in the racing office gives them a calendar. They all got a winner's circle photo and not a one asked if we made any money. Tell you the truth, I really don't think they care."

He fished a check out of his wallet and unfolded it for her.

"Wow," she said. "Reggie."

"He and his friends just bought our chestnut mare, the one that broke her maiden last week. She beat a bad bunch, making her worth about twenty-five so I asked for a hundred. Thought he'd counter but he didn't blink."

"Think he's marking it up?"

"Don't know and don't care. Made me kick him back five percent, but that's what you have to pay an agent, so who cares. And he's been talking to me about starting his own stable. Take me up to Kentucky in his plane and maybe buy a bunch of yearlings at Keeneland in September."

"He's got a plane?"

"Lear jet I think. At that part of the airport where they keep the private planes."

"I think he's creepy. Daddy said never trust men who wear pinky rings or bow ties unless they're in a tuxedo."

"Ah, he's just different. He says he's expecting to be made the president of that bank pretty soon. Brought a big car dealer to the barn with him. And he's having lunch with the governor this week."

"Creepy," she said.

~~

The sun was just cracking the horizon and the track kitchen was nearly deserted when Joe paid for his breakfast, a *Daily Racing Form* and the local gazette. He transferred his plate and coffee cup from the tray to one of the small green Formica-topped tables near the door and unfolded the paper.

"Shit," he said, a little too loudly.

There was a fairly unflattering photo of Reginald White, likely taken upon his arrest, under the headline that read: BANK JOB!

Joe read the article as far as the part that told how Reginald was a teller who had tapped the People's Trust for just almost half a million before they caught him and stopped reading when the article started to detail how there would be a full investigation into what he'd done with the cash. But there was evidence he had been buying racehorses with some of it and creating a Ponzi scheme.

The last words Joe read were the police chief's, saying there was a possibility that dozens had been taken, buying into Reginald's swindle and vowing that all the scammers would soon be behind bars.

~~

The cop turned the page on his yellow legal pad. He squirmed to get comfortable in a hard plastic chair that barely contained his overweight frame, but he was nearing full retirement and willing to put up with any assignment as long as it didn't involve physical effort.

"So, Joe Turner, age fifty, married, with two daughters. You're a driver at the horse track."

"No," said Turner. "I was. And it's jockey, not driver. Drivers are for harness racing. What I did was ride Thoroughbreds."

"Okay, so you're a jockey," said the cop, touching the point of his pencil to his tongue before he scrawled.

"No, I *was* a jockey. I retired five years ago. Now I'm a trainer. Used to ride them, now I train them."

That draws a blank stare from the officer before he makes his notes.

"I went to the races once with my old man. Yonkers, I think it was. They ran at night and he used to go all the time. I remember my ma bitching at him 'cause he always lost."

"Yeah, that's different, harness racing. What I do is with the Thoroughbreds. Like Secretariat? The Standardbreds have a sulky behind them, Thoroughbreds have a jockey that rides them. Two different things."

"Okay, yeah, Secretariat," said the cop. "All horses though, right. Basically the same thing. They go around in a circle and you can bet on them. They're mostly fixed they say, right? Like boxing, all mobbed up?"

He makes some more notes and takes no notice of Joe's frustration.

"So you quit being a … jockey, and now you're a trainer."

"I retired," said Joe.

"Kind of young for retirement."

"One spill too many."

"So it's like a retirement job. Like part time?"

Joe laughed, starting to feel like he's trying to swim upstream.

"Part time like seven days a week. Horses need looking after like kids, every day, every night. You have to be crazy to do this job."

The cop makes more notes, relaxed and drinking coffee from a Styrofoam cup.

"You make a lot of money at that?" he says.

"If you get a good one," says Joe.

"Got any good ones?"

"Not really. We had a filly that won almost three hundred thousand two years ago, but nothing since."

"Three hundred thousand, wow. You made that from one horse?"

"No, we get ten percent of what they make. The owner gets the rest."

Joe could see the number 300 with a big circle around it that the cop had penciled in the middle of the page. He knew that was all the cop had gotten, that Joe made three hundred thousand bucks and the rest of their conversation went in one ear and out the other.

"Okay, so tell me how you know Reginald White," said the cop.

~~

Donald Shea, Attorney at Law was etched in the glass door. A blue-haired receptionist was filing a fingernail and didn't notice them come in. Joe and Lilly were side by side, holding hands when Joe told her they had an appointment, but they were early.

"He'll see you in a minute," she said and after about forty-five minutes she took them in. Joe was distracted by the amount of diplomas and accolades covering the wall of the lawyer's office.

"The way it looks," said Donald, "your chance is about twenty-five percent. Of being convicted on all counts."

"Three to one – great," Joe said to Lilly. "Three to one is usually the favorite. I'm the favorite to go to jail. One time I'd like to be a longshot."

"The problem we have is whatever deal the D.A. is going to cut with White. He's clearly culpable but he's going to try and lay some of the blame off on you in exchange for them giving him a break. They haven't found most of the half-million he stole, but that check for a hundred grand looks like you were in on the pyramid he created. Especially since you wrote him a stable check for five thousand, and the prosecution will take you along as collateral damage in any event. They'll tie the two of you together and make you the brains since it was a horse scheme. Make it look like you were laundering the money he stole and bury you along with him, only he'll get the break and you'll get the beating."

"I thought he was a rich guy – didn't have any idea he was a bank robber," said Joe.

Lilly let go of his hand.

"I told you he was creepy."

"The fact that you were selling more than a hundred percent of a horse sure makes you look like you weren't above doing something dishonest. That's what they're going to try and convince the jury."

"He's the one that stole the money. Told me to hold the check for a hundred for a couple of days while he moved money. In the meantime, he cashed mine and when I deposited his it bounced."

"That's not what he's going to say. He's going to say you sold him a share and told him how to make a bundle peddling small pieces to other people. You're going to be Ponzi and he's just a poor bank teller you seduced into being a degenerate gambler. They have video of him betting twenty thousand on one of your horses. And plenty of pictures of the two of you at the track. They're still finding money missing. And he might have cracked a few safe deposit boxes too."

"I didn't even think he bet."

"Yeah, well he sure did, but he didn't pick too many winners. Out of the half-million they were only able to find about thirty thousand."

~~

Lilly and the girls stood with their backs against the mom-van, watching Joe as he exited the prison gate. They waited until he was almost to the car before the three of them ran to him and they all embraced for what seemed like a long time. Joe took a look back at the stone walls and spit in the direction of the gate before he got in the passenger side of the car. He covered Lilly's hand with his on the shift knob and closed his eyes after she told the girls to be quiet and stop asking questions, your Daddy's had a long day. They stayed on the interstate for nearly four hours until they passed the church they went to every Sunday and when they turned the corner on Broad Street, Joe asked her to pull in at the 7-Eleven.

"Sounds stupid, but I been dying for a Gatorade for two years," he said. He got halfway to the store when he realized he had no money, nothing in his pockets, and came back to the car. Lilly gave him a twenty-dollar bill and he returned with his drink and a bag full of candy that he passed to the girls in the back seat.

It was dark by the time they got home and Lilly turned off the car and they all sat there in the driveway, quiet and staring at the house. Lilly sent the girls upstairs to do their homework while she started dinner. Joe played in the back yard with their dog Duffy for a while, throwing a tennis ball until the old Lab gave up and laid at his feet and when he came inside, he went to the refrigerator, just out of habit.

"I made that chicken pot-pie you like," said Lilly.

"Yeah, then I better get to bed, I got to get up and mow some grass tomorrow," he said.

AT THE END OF THE BAR

Weaver closed the loan document, slid it into a file folder, and tossed it in the basket at the corner of his desk, then found a paper napkin to wipe the sweat from his forehead. The thermostat was set to 68 and a floor fan droned in the corner, but the noonday sun pressed its heat right through the reflective film on the picture window with a view of the parking lot, and as much as he tried to cool the room, it was no use.

He put the cap back on the pricey black fountain pen his brother-in-law had given him as a birthday gift and placed it in its usual spot in the tray of the desk drawer next to the track program he saved from the time they went to the Kentucky Derby. The pen and program were joined by a pair of souvenir dice from a trip to Vegas and a worn Eisenhower silver dollar that he sometimes used to cap his cards when he played poker.

He picked up the Eisenhower and recalled the last time he'd played a couple of months before at the Indian casino. He'd gone all-in for his last two hundred with a set of sevens, and a kid with a nose ring and dime-sized earring holes made an inside straight on the river and went cavorting around the room, celebrating like he'd just won the World Series of Poker.

Weaver stared at the framed photo of his wife and kids on his desk for a few moments before he slipped the coin into his watch pocket and closed the drawer. He knew the urge was going to get to him and made no attempt to ignore it. He picked up the picture and held it for a few moments before he placed it face down on his desk and made for the door.

Outside, the Arizona heat hit him full force and he fumbled for the cheap pair of shades he'd bought the day before from a rack at the Walgreens. He paused at the marble fountain with a statue of some Navajo chieftain that had been dry since the city turned off the water and threw in a handful of coins that bounced off the white tiles pockmarked with stains from pennies tossed by previous supplicants to the gods of luck.

Feeling peckish, Weaver detoured around the corner to the handcart of the old man who peddled dirty-water hotdogs and German sausages every day at lunchtime. There were six in line ahead of him. He calculated at least a minute and a half for each transaction and decided it wasn't worth wasting the ten minutes. Not for a dirty-water dog.

Instead, Weaver found sanctuary in his usual spot at the end of the long wooden bar in the Tall Saguaro Tavern. In the corner there, near the front door, he could see everyone in the place if he bothered to look. He ordered a whiskey and a draft. A Red Breast and a lager.

"Like anything today, Weave?" asked the bartender.

His name was Norman. He pushed across a *Racing Form* open to the day's entries at Turf Paradise. On flat-screen TVs attached to two of the walls, horses paraded to the post above the colored numbers indicating their odds as talking heads tried to encourage viewers to make their bets.

Weaver shrugged and sipped his beer. While Norm was distracted by a customer, he picked up the *Form* and cringed when he saw the barkeep's cryptic scratchings in blue and red. Weaver hated that. He hated to see another gambler's notes in case they might influence his own thoughts, or even worse, agree with them, in which case the horse never won. He pushed the paper aside and downed the whiskey.

At a ratty old pool table toward the back of the room a couple bickered as the man flipped a coin to see who'd break. The table was an antique three slate with stained green felt and mesh leather pockets, lucky to have survived the hurricane of 1900 at Harvey's Saloon on the Galveston Strand before riding west in the bed of a pickup truck. There was a black and white framed photo of the flooded Texas street on the wall next to the cue rack, testifying to the table's legacy.

"Heads you break," said the guy.

His arms were too scrawny for his tank top, displaying multiple tattoos faded from the desert sun. His face had more cracks than an old catcher's mitt, making him look a dozen years older than he probably was. The coin fell heads and the girl took the cue ball. She was his physical opposite, no youngster either, but you could tell she was buff under the Lakers sweatshirt. She sank two balls on the break.

"You got stripes again, Maury," she said. "You'll probably be in stripes again soon."

She laughed at her own joke that Maury never heard. He was watching a race on the flat-screen and moaned when the horse on the lead got nipped at the wire.

"Damn," he said.

"All horseplayers die broke," she said.

Norman was back to refill Weaver's glass without being asked.

"Kelly likes his in the fifth, I hear," said Norman.

Weaver let it fall without comment and downed his drink.

"My wife left," he said.

It was the first personal thing he'd shared after a decade on the same barstool.

"Sorry," said the barkeep.

"Not your fault, Normie," said Weaver, fishing for his wallet. He left a twenty and a ten and headed for the door.

Sitting in his eight-year-old Audi, waiting for the AC to kick in and the light to change, he wondered if Janet was in Boston yet and if the kids missed him. He figured it was inevitable she would tell them what a lousy father he had been, and what a deadbeat loser he was. But what did she expect? she'd said. He'd taken her to the track on their first date, to a casino on their second, and lost everything in his pockets both times.

The light turned green and the driver behind him honked his horn, just enough to annoy. Weaver pulled away slowly, just enough to exact a petty revenge.

As he drove his mind continued to wander. Where it was that he had been going? Norm's bar?

No, been there. The poker room? Home? Oh yeah, the racetrack. He thought it was good of her to have waited until the kids were out of school for the summer before she told him she was done.

~~

The track offered some solace and Weaver was feeling fine right up to the moment he ate a hot dog following the eighth race. It was well done, off one of those rolling grills, and there was a good chance it might have been simmering there since yesterday's late double. He had loaded it with yellow mustard, chopped onions, and dill relish, and took his time taking small bites while tearing off the excess bun and tossing it in the trashcan.

On one of the simulcast TV screens, Earlie Fires had just won wire-to-wire going a mile and a sixteenth to give Weaver four winners in a row in the Arlington Park Pick Six. Weaver's heady thoughts of a huge score were dulled by the gas pain rising in his chest. He wondered if they sold Tums in the gift shop. He made a few failed attempts at a cleansing belch before the thickness at the top of his chest got worse and rose to his collarbone.

A fellow punter noted the remnant of hot dog on Weaver's empty paper plate.

"How's the pups today?" he said.

"Just the right amount of yesterday's grease," said Weaver, rubbing his collarbone.

He popped the last bite in his mouth, tossed the plate, and started down the back stairs toward the paddock. But for some reason the stairs became soft and squishy and the handrail hot to the touch. He heard a high, wailing sound in the distance. He thought, *I better sit down before I fall down,* only he wasn't sure who he was talking about.

Weaver opened his eyes to find himself sitting on the floor, his back against the wall. He shook his head in an attempt to clear the cobwebs and squinted at the annoying fluorescent lighting overhead, only it seemed as if the walls were lighted the same as the ceiling. Someone with a firm grip grabbed his hand and pulled him to his feet. Weaver was confronted by an older gent in a grey top hat, red waistcoat, and tan jodhpurs.

"Thanks," said Weaver. His chest hurt like he'd been kicked by a horse. "What the hell are you, the bugler?"

He tried to escape the man's vise-like grip, but to no avail.

"Used to be," he said. "I worked backup for the horn-blower at Narragansett and Suffolk in the forties. Now I'm just your friendly guide to the other side. Call me Sid. Come on just down this hall and

I'll check you in. Nasty heart attack you had. I bet those things hurt like a bugger."

He let go of Weaver's hand and started down the corridor.

"What do you mean, heart attack?" said Weaver. "Check me in where? Other side of what?"

"Basically, friend, you just threw snake-eyes leaving the mezzanine, crapped out on the way down the stairs, and now you're headed to Horse Heaven, the Great Racetrack in the Sky – all those clever names they call it. You might want to put your sunglasses on. Everybody hates the harsh lighting in this hallway. I think that's where all the 'white light' stuff got started."

"Wait. No wait," said Weaver, hanging back. "This is some kind of a mistake."

"You'd be surprised how many times I hear that," said Sid. "Actually, you were marginal to get in at all, but we had a spot open today, so I took you off the waiting list from Gambler's Purgatory. Came down to you and a guy at Walmart that got run over by a forklift. He was listening to hip hop on his head-phones and scratching off a lottery ticket when it happened. Never felt a thing, but even so, situations like that are why we got a list."

Weaver stared, open-mouthed.

"Most any other time I doubt you'd have made the cut," Sid went on. "Not really a lot of redeeming qualities on your curriculum vitae. You could have ended up in the Degenerates level of Gamblers' Purgatory. You wouldn't have liked it there. Those guys never pick a winner, and even when they do it gets taken down. I assume you're good with this."

He pointed at the door at the end of the tunnel, framed with garish neon. He showed Weaver an iPad, its screen a jumble of words.

"Good with it?" said Weaver. "Good with what?"

"Horse Heaven, instead of the alternatives," said Sid. "Although you don't really look like a jockey."

Weaver was close to a panic attack.

"What do you mean, a jockey?" he said. "I never sat on a horse in my life!"

Sid frowned and consulted his iPad.

"Well now, it's all right here," he said. "You're Raul Jimenez, age fifty-five, ex-jockey and exercise boy. Worked at a carwash when he wasn't riding horses. Threw up a lot and took too many diet pills to make the weight and still you binged on Haagen-Daz. That's why you had the heart attack. Lousy diet and too much cholesterol."

"Heart attack?" said Weaver, feeling his wounded chest.

Sid tapped the iPad.

"It's all right here."

Weaver looked down the tunnel. The door with the neon was standing wide open. He took a step toward Sid and pointed a thumb at himself.

"Walter James Weaver, age fifty-five," he said. "Chases dead-beats for a savings and loan. Drinks a lot and bets on way too many losers. Check and see if that's in your computer, 'cause *that's* who I am."

Sid swiped his screen and read further on. His mouth twisted in an embarrassed frown.

"Oh, shit to high heaven," he said, shaking his head. "Pardon my French. Lemme check if it's too late."

A viewing window appeared on the hallway wall through which Weaver could see a busy hospital emergency room where half a dozen surgeons in bright white scrubs surrounded an operating table. The body on the table was wearing a blue-checked dress shirt identical to the one Weaver donned before he left his house at 8:30 that morning. A nurse pulled the sheet over the patient's head.

"What? No!" Weaver said. "Are you saying that's me under the sheet? Done? Finito?"

"I'm really sorry," said Sid. "Nothing I can do once they make it official."

"Fucking stewards!" said Weaver. "But it's your fault. What a shitty call! And I'm alive four-by-four in the Pick Six at Arlington."

"That's not really an expression we use here," said Sid.

"You know how hard it is to be live with four in a row after nailing two 20-to-1 shots and no favorites," said Weaver.

He pointed at Sid's iPad.

"The fifth leg of the Six must be over by now," said Weaver. "Can you just tell me who won?"

"That I can do," said Sid, tapping one of his apps. "Here we go. Pat Day wins it! We love Pat here."

"I'll be damned," said Weaver.

Sid raised an eyebrow.

"Mister Dabaday," said Weaver. "I had him. Five-to-one, morning line. What about the last? I'm live to four horses in there, too."

"Post time's not for ten minutes," said Sid. "That's almost an eternity here. Anyway, I can tell you what happened in the past, but the future we stay out of. That's what we have touts for."

"You mean you can bet horses in heaven?" said Weaver.

"There's as many horseplayers in Horse Heaven as there are chess players in hell," said Sid. "You'll like it."

Weaver considered for a moment, then shook his head.

"Nah, you gotta try and get me back," said Weaver. "With the three-day carryover, this could be the best day of my life. If I were alive, that is. Go find that Jimenez guy was supposed to be me. Or give that Walmart stiff a break. It's your mistake."

The old man shook his head.

"Great," said Weaver. "My wife leaves with the kids 'cause I'm always broke and you ice me by mistake when I'm about to make a life changing score. What a day."

"Very sorry," said the old man.

"How about I promise if I hit to put ten percent in the basket at church on Sunday?" said Weaver.

"Really," said Sid, again giving him the eyebrow.

"Twenty percent," said Weaver.

The old man scanned his iPad again.

"Last time you were in church was 1992," he said.

"I never knew which one to go to," said Weaver. "Half Jewish, half Catholic. You sure that's not Jimenez?"

"It's not open to negotiation," said Sid.

"Okay, thirty percent," said Weaver. "Put that thing away. You're worse than my bookie."

"Why don't we go watch your race?" said Sid.

Another door opened and they were standing at the outside rail of a pristine racetrack with perfect harrow lines as the horses in the post parade approached.

"We're live to the 2-3-4 and 7," said Weaver. "Four gets the whole pool."

Sid handed him a new pair of Bushnell 10x50 binoculars.

"A welcome gift," he said.

Weaver noticed that even after the horses paraded past, the track was still unmarked. He decided to ignore that and focused on the starting gate. The horses broke unevenly, more than half the field three or four lengths behind after a few strides, as the two leaders ding-donged on the lead. Weaver lowered the binoculars and checked the numbers on the big-screen board hovering six feet off the ground in the infield. Number 7 was edging away from the 2, 3 and 4. With about hundred yards to go, though, Weaver could see the 7 begin to labor while the others were gaining ground with every stride. When they hit the wire, all he could hear was the announcer exclaiming, "Too close to call," as the big-screen flashed in giant red letters, PHOTO!

"You got it," said Sid.

"Damn right I got it," said Weaver. "But which one?"

~~

"Whoa!" said Weaver, responding to the ampule of amyl nitrite cracked open under his nose. He sat bolt upright against the wall as an EMT slid a blood pressure cuff on his left arm.

"I had a heart attack," said Weaver.

"Nah, you were choking on a hot dog," said the EMT. "She saved your bacon with a Heimlich and you passed out."

A little old white-haired lady standing nearby gave Weaver a wan smile and a wave like the Queen of England.

"Learned it on YouTube, dearie," she said. "You were my first."

Weaver clutched his chest.

"Pain?" said the EMT.

Weaver produced a mutual ticket from the breast pocket of his shirt.

"Nah, it's my ticket," he said.

The EMT finished packing his equipment.

"Check with your GP if you have any issues," said the EMT. "As far as that goes, you've already had a winning day."

~~

The last race of the Pick Six at Arlington was official, but sometimes it takes a few minutes to crunch the numbers and announce the winners and consolations. Not on this day, though. There was one lucky horseplayer who took down the whole six-winner pool, who placed his bet out West at Turf Paradise.

The teller arranged the hundred dollar-bills in neat stacks of ten thousand dollars each then he re-banded them.

"There's one hundred thirty-eight thousand, four hundred twenty-six," said the teller. "Let me get you a bag."

Weaver scooped up the cash and left a tip of one-twenty-six.

"Thanks," said the teller. "Hope to see you again soon."

This time Weaver knew exactly where he was going. After parking the Audi in the driveway, he could see the front door of his house was ajar. He pushed it open and stepped in quietly. His daughter and son were on the couch in the TV room, playing a video game and never taking their eyes off the screen.

"Where's Mom?" he asked.

The little girl shrugged her shoulders, and the boy nodded toward the kitchen.

His wife, on her cellphone, offered a small wave and a quick grin.

"He's home, Ma," she said. "I'll talk to you tomorrow."

"Hello," said Weaver. "I thought you were going."

He had become unaware of the bag of money dangling from his hand like a sack of dirty laundry.

"No," she said, "I guess you're stuck with me. Or I'm stuck with you."

"But you said – "

"I know what I said, and I meant it when I did," she said. "But everybody deserves a second chance. Maybe even a third."

Weaver felt something in his chest that was neither pain nor pressure.

"Besides," she said. "I figure one of these days your luck will turn around."

SELL CIGARETTES?

It's late afternoon at the Dew Drop Inn, but you can never tell what time it is since there are no windows save the small ones at each end of the shoe-box shaped room and the one at the front of the building by the pool table with raggedy stars and stripes curtains that haven't let in any light since they went up before the Vietnam War.

The temperature in Tucson gets to one-fifteen when the summer solstice aims the sun directly at Arizona, so no one begrudges me the cave-like decor since part of the place's appeal is its first-class air conditioning. We used to think I was building a nest egg so Monica and I could go back to Jersey when the kids were grown, but as it turns out they're both back at the Shore raising our grandkids and we're still here.

Slim, who's more or less the mayor of the joint, has to make an effort to haul all of his hundred and eight pounds onto a barstool to begin laboring over a dog track program like it was the Manhattan Project. He has a pinched little ski-jump nose like

Bob Hope and a permanent curve in his upper lip that makes it look like he's halfway grinning at something all the time.

"Sell cigarettes here, Jackie?" he says, peering over the cheater specs he got for six bucks at the car wash.

"Thought you were trying to quit," I say, pointing to the ancient vending machine by the men's room door, still in the same spot where it landed when my old man opened the place after he dragged the family out here in '62.

He studies the distance between himself and the smokes.

"None behind the bar, eh?"

It's a game we play. I shake out one of my Marlboros and slide it to him along with my lighter.

"What are you drinking today?"

"Is it summer or winter?"

"August would still be summer."

"Rum it in the summer, whiskey it in the winter. Give me some of that Bajan, Mister Church style."

"Two cubes, three fingers," I say to confirm.

He swirls the rum around the glass before draining half in the first gulp.

"You're pretty chipper," I say.

"How far to the dog track?" says Slim.

"About six miles, as if you don't know. Something must be up there. You're the fourth person today, talking about it."

Besides the pups, the only gambling action between here and Vegas is Turf Paradise in Phoenix and Rillito Park here for the horses, but Rillito hardly runs anymore since the Indians started opening casinos everywhere.

"That's 'cause money draws a crowd, pal," Slim says. "There's a three-day carryover in the Pick Six – thirty-two grand. I just got my Social Security, and I got a theory."

"Hey, what a coincidence, I got a drawer full of IOUs from guys with some of those very same theories."

"No really, we should have a swing at it," says Slim.

He empties the glass and looks into it like a fortune teller contemplating a crystal ball.

"I have trouble picking one in a row, let alone six," I say.

"That's horses you tried," he says. "Dogs are a lot easier. Only eight in each race and no jockeys to fuck it up. We put in a couple-hundred-dollar ticket and we can cover all the likelies, and I guarantee you none of those low-rent losers that hang out there is taking anything bigger than a twenty-dollar stab. It's a matter of evaluating the competition, almost more than handicapping."

He taps his temple as if it were the repository of vast knowledge and motions for a refill, since he's now starting to like the sound of his own pitch.

"You work tonight, Jackie?" he says.

"Off at seven."

"I'll drive," he says.

I spend a minute pondering the bar's Budweiser promo lamp – the one with a team of tiny plastic Clydesdales pulling the beer wagon inside – before I weaken.

"There's nothing on TV. Laundry's done. Okay, you drive."

~~

We pull into the greyhound track and there's only about a hundred cars in the lot. A tumbleweed blows past on the cracked asphalt and misses them all.

"It's a lot smaller than a real track," I say, looking around once inside.

"Horses," Slim says, holding a hand eye level, then holding it two feet off the ground. "Dogs."

The Pick Six doesn't start until the fifth race, so we hang at the rail, watching handlers stuff flea-bitten greyhounds into the starting boxes before the doors pop up and they fly out to chase a metal rabbit on a rail, once white as the Easter Bunny but now, with age, a forlorn Bugs Bunny grey. Winning favorites abound, and the crowd's enthusiasm level is somewhere between a silent movie and a wake.

We put in a $234 ticket, playing program choices and singling a couple of morning-line four-to-five shots that look like they can't get beat, since it's our first swing, after which we watch helplessly as the first one wipes out on the clubhouse turn and doesn't even finish. The next four get home first for us before the last one lopes home second, so we don't even get the consolation payoff for picking five out of six.

"Not as easy as it looks," says Slim, stroking his chin whiskers.

It's almost midnight as we're trudging out the exit with the other stiffs when I complain what a waste that was, and Slim says I told you it might take a few tries to get the hang of it and don't be such a mope.

"Look at it this way, we had four outta six and we don't even know what we're doing," he says. "Anyway, nobody picked six, so it carries over again. We'll hit it tomorrow, get our money back and everybody else's too. You have to work tomorrow?"

"I don't know about this. I'm not a big fan of throwing good money after bad."

"It's what you call a learning curve," Slim says. "But maybe we could find somebody here, already knows what they're doing, and pay them to get their picks."

When I point out that if those guys could pick winners why wouldn't they do it for themselves, Slim nods towards the dispirited customers climbing into their rusted-out jalopies.

"Like I said, look at these guys. Crumb-bums who couldn't buy a six-dollar combo ticket let alone invest a C-note. Even I feel like a high-roller here. Maybe for a code name call me Mister Dandalos."

I give him a look.

"You know. Nick the Greek," he says. "That was his real name, Nick Dandalos."

I give him the same look and get in his car.

We're halfway back to town when Slim lights the joint he's had stuck in his hatband all night. He offers me a hit, but I decline.

"Let's ask around," he says, "What we need is a picker. Call it a little R & D."

~~

The next night we get there early and start to feel out a few locals. Most of them put on a bashful act except one guy in a Hawaiian shirt with blond hair who says his name is Whitey - what a surprise - and looks every bit the part of what you'd imagine a dog track degenerate in his late sixties would be.

"Here's what we're thinking," Slim says to him.

Whitey is chewing gum and tapping a foot.

"We don't really know the puppies that well and you're here every day. Maybe you help us with some smart picks when we put together a big ticket and we'll give you a grand if it wins."

"Sounds good to me," says Whitey, chewing and tapping.

He goes off to handicap, comes back a little later and gives us three picks in each race for the entire card which will cost us over seven hundred for a Pick Six ticket. He asks for a small advance and looks disappointed when we turn him down, so Slim buys him a beer and a bag of chips and we grab some seats in the grandstand bleachers and watch our dogs win the first five races. We're counting our money, but then the last one gets beat a nose by a forty-to-one shot, so we're out nearly a grand, but at least nobody hits for six, which means another carry-over. We slip Whitey the ninety-six bucks we get back for the consolation and tell him to do better tomorrow.

Tomorrow comes with its Pick Six topped out at $41,000 and we take down the whole pool with the only winning ticket. The hounds are barely across the finish line when Whitey starts whining he needs more money, that he ain't doing all the work and getting peanuts, since it's all him picking these winners and only getting a grand for being a genius. We point out that his overhead thus far has been a Bic pen, and we bought him the program. We tell him a deal's a deal and he can have two G's if he does it again, but a third of the pie is out of the question. He says up yours, gimmie my G-whiz, and I quit.

Slim says no problem, Whitey wasn't a genius in any shape or form, and in less than ten minutes here comes a kid wearing a backwards ball cap and a Breaking Bad t-shirt asking if we're looking for a new picker because he heard about Whitey, who's an asshole anyway. The kid says he can pick better than Whitey any day of the week and a grand is just peachy.

The track is only open Friday through Sunday, but by the end of the next week there's another Pick Six carry-over and we catch it for 35K. A fortnight later we nail another for 28K and we pitch the kid an extra two G's both times and he's happy as a fat guy with a free roll at the Chinese all-you-can-eat buffet, and besides we get an extra kick since you just know he's going to rib Whitey on top of it.

~~

This fine madness goes on for about two months, us ordinary stiffs working the mutt-garden like it's our own personal Fort Knox, and we start considering maybe we should list ourselves as professional gamblers on next year's tax return.

One day Slim hops up on the barstool with the spring of a high school hurdler and lights a Tiparillo, then pulls his dog track program from an alligator attaché case and slaps it on the bar.

"Carry-ov-ah, baby," he says. "Thirty Geezlestones."

By now he has taken to wearing a black straw hasty-brim and a good-luck horseshoe pinky ring with a half-carat diamond in its center. I, on the other hand, deferring to discretion and not wishing to alert the populace of my newly found prosperity, never depart from a lifelong personal style of plain gray Sansabelt Stay Press slacks and a short-sleeved white no-iron. My profits shall go undetected by anyone other than those guys at Scotttrade who might have noticed my investment in a Nicaraguan oil field that my ex-brother-in-law assures me will be the next Exxon.

"New shirt?" I ask.

"Tommy Bahama. Their stuff is perfect for guys with my build," says Slim. "You should try it."

"You're a walking fashion statement," I say. "I'm a Big and Tall guy, myself. Whiskey?"

"Make it a double Jameson, I'm feeling lucky."

At this juncture it should be noted that Maury at the end of the bar, who is never heard to speak even should a natural disaster of mammoth proportions be taking place, looks up from his sports page, takes a slug of the draft he's been nursing for an hour while grazing free on my shell-em-yourself peanuts, and announces:

"According to the scribe in here they're gonna cancel the Pick Six after tonight. Says they decided the same guys keep hitting it and it ain't fair."

Our eyes lock in near terror as Slim downs the Jameson while I whip off my apron and tell the cook to close up as we head out the door faster than the hounds leave the box.

~~

We must have been in the dog track's business office half-a-dozen times in the past three months, collecting our winnings and getting schmoozed by a management rightfully under the impression that big-time gamblers like us should always be treated as a version of Vegas whales, wined and dined and regularly showered with perks like free programs, beers, and hot dogs.

But apparently the prevailing winds are no longer from Vichy. Murphy the GM is now getting his marching orders from somewhere else.

"You guys are hurting the handle," he says. "The regular customers resent you coming in and scooping the pot after they build it up. It's over, done. Tonight's the last night."

"But last week you said we were good for business, Murph-ski," says Slim. "We been betting fifteen hundred into the pool and losing some nights when nobody else bet a C-note, dude."

Murphy's distaste for the familiarity is painted across his kisser.

"Somebody's got to hit it," I add.

"Somebody can hit it someplace else," says Murphy. "Try boxing some trifectas. There's the door."

Slim stands, helpless and groping for a comeback.

"That's a hell of a way to do business," he snarls.

I am compelled to add my two cents worth of empty threat.

"And you just lost ours."

As we make our way through the grandstand, Slim is now feeling the full effect of the joint he smoked in the car on the way over and he looks like he's either going to cry or puke. We pass Whitey, who flashes a stupid smile like the Joe Peschi character in one of those kid-left-behind movies and gives us the finger.

Our picker is waiting at the usual spot, his new leather Breaking Bad varsity jacket buttoned all the way to his chin like maybe he's cold.

"They can't do that, can they?" he says "Isn't that restraint of trade like the Laurel and Hartley Act, or something like that," proving correct my suspicion that a little bit of schooling can be dangerous.

"Feel lucky?" I ask, as the kid proffers his sweat-stained program.

"You're in for a third if we hit tonight," says Slim, and we slog to the second floor to our usual spot to watch as the picks go six-for-six when half a dozen favorites win in a row and we have the pleasure of sharing the pool with 173 other lucky patrons who hit for $154 each and we only lose twelve-hundred on the night.

~~

It's quiet in Slim's new Bimmer 540 at least halfway home before either one of us can speak when I finally comment on the car.

"Very sporty. Must have cost a pretty penny."

"Nobody pays cash anymore. Everybody leases, so you can write it off. Much more affordable way to ride. Only nine-ninety a month."

That's when he reveals to me that he's slightly overextended and asks me if I'm still flush enough for a short-term loan, and when I ask him how much cash he's got left I can tell by the way he looks a little green around the gills there's a good chance he's in possession of next to nothing that folds.

"Uncle Sammy's withholding took a big chunk and then there was the down stroke for the car, plus what I sent my old lady in Tahoe to cover her rent," he says. "And the new duds, dressing for success. Maybe I got another G-whiz in my sock drawer."

I knew he was lying.

"Maybe less," he confesses.

"How much to dump the car lease?" I say, avoiding the subject of dry holes in the Nicaraguan oil fields.

"Why would I do that?" he asks.

"Unless you've got another theory," I say, "don't ask me to front for lottery tickets again."

"It coulda worked," says Slim as we pull up in front of the Inn.

~~

I don't see Slim for a couple of months, until one afternoon he materializes on his stool at the bar like an apparition.

"Look at this," he says.

He has a copy of the *Las Vegas Review-Journal* sports section with the headline over racing writer Rich Eng's column, "Quarter-Million Dollar Carry-over in Turf Paradise Super High Five."

"Great, here we go again," I say.

"Five G's and change and we can cover the field. We can't lose."

"Wasn't that what you told me about the oh-eight Super Bowl? Best team since the Shula Dolphins?' I didn't finish paying off that bookie until last August."

He chuckles and asks if I want to hear a joke, but it's clear I've got no choice.

"You hear about the two guys at the track? They drop twenty-grand and the last race is over and they're walking out, and one guy says, 'Let's go to the dog track and try to get even.' The other guy looks at him like he's crazy and says, 'Dogs? What do I know about betting dogs?'"

"You're kind of making my point, only in reverse," I say.

"This is different," says Slim. "It's simple math. We're dealing with just one race, twelve horses in the field. One is a cinch, two others look to finish second or third on paper but one of them can't possibly hit the board 'cause he's trained by a guy who never wins and ridden by a ten-pound bug who hasn't won his first race yet. He'll have trouble finishing last, let alone in the first five. We just take the cinch on top and box the other ten under him. It's a once-in-a-lifetime deal. We hit and we quit. I swear."

"Is this for a comedy show and I'm being taped?" I say. "Like I don't know that every time you leave just one out, that's the one that comes in and screws you?"

"Nah. It's five-grand and forty bucks. Covering the other one is throwing away almost three thou' we don't have."

"Which is much better than the five-grand that we don't have in the first place," I point out.

"Exactly," says Slim. "Never throw good money after bad."

~~

It's late afternoon at the Dew Drop Inn and I'm having to wear sunglasses because the new picture windows I installed let in too much light, even with the tinting and the curtains with the tropical motif Slim's girlfriend designed. I haven't seen either of them since we split the winnings from the Super High Five, so it's a surprise when I hear his voice.

"Sell cigarettes here, Jackie?"

ALLSHEWROTE

Loretta liked to sit at the bar of the Trail's End Tavern and watch Zane as he sliced the limes into small squares that would fit perfectly in the neck of the Mexican bottled beer. She would sit there and read the obituaries in the *Arizona Star* with her back to the door just like her father always told her not to. Her old man was an Italian from Staten Island and grew up watching the "Godfather Saga" over and over, always thinking some mobster hitmen were going to burst in the door at any minute and spray the place with bullets. Loretta didn't buy that, being pretty sure that not many insurance salesmen from the suburbs who drove Chevy Impalas like her father and played golf on the weekend were on the Mafia's rub-out list just because their name ended in a vowel.

Zane topped her glass with Bud Light from the tap, his with Coors, and they clinked glasses as they shared the last of a bag of potato chips while he tuned the TVs to the various sports channels. They weren't typical Arizonians of the lily-white pioneer persuasion – Zane with his Roman nose, jet black hair and dark brown eyes, Loretta an olive-skinned beauty right out of Brooklyn – but they both had personalities that lit up a room, and they could fit in anywhere.

The same could be said for the two older Black gents who were semi-regulars at the Trail's End, as long as "anywhere" was a racetrack like little Rillito Park on the outskirts of Tucson. Known as Rodney the Clocker and Blinky the Valet, they would plant themselves on the well-worn bench under a live oak a few yards from the saddling paddock and sit for hours, close together, leaning in to compensate for a mutual loss of hearing.

Rodney could best be described as taciturn, preferring to withhold his council on all but the most pressing topics. His hair was sprinkled with grey, and he wore white, button-downed dress shirts, starched and pressed to within an inch of their natural lives. Blinky, by contrast, was the talker, animated to the point of jumping to his feet and waving his arms to make his case. His hair had gone nearly all white with just a fringe of black at the temples, and his daily wardrobe always included a blue chambray long-sleeve, usually frayed at the collar and never introduced to an iron.

Zane connected naturally with characters like Rodney and Blinky. As a little kid back in Brooklyn, on most Saturday afternoons his mother Ida would watch the family bar on Fort Hamilton Parkway while his old man took him on the train to Aqueduct. They'd paper a couple of seats on the third floor and spend the day trying to pick winners. Zane's old man loved a jockey named Hedley Woodhouse. He followed Hedley for years and his son Bobby Woodhouse, too, when he started riding. Not household names, but they brought in plenty of what Angelo Rocco and his kid were looking for – longshots.

Once the Roccos moved West, Zane had worked tending bar for his old man most of the time after he finished school until the track deal came up at Rillito from a friend's father who was on the racing commission. They needed someone who could cook and run a counter and didn't have an arrest record. That was him, so he was out on his own.

The track wasn't like anywhere else Zane had ever been. Sometimes he wondered if he hadn't run away and joined the circus, slinging hash for colorful Damon Runyon characters. And it was just like the circus in many ways. Jockeys were the little people and the high wire acts, trainers trained horses instead of lions, and plenty of the rest made up the cast of clowns and freaks.

Rillito featured an oval of only five furlongs, what the racing guys called a "bullring" for obvious reasons, and the purses were correspondingly small. It seemed like the local horse folks ran fixed races more often than not, but it was the only action for many miles, so what the hell.

Because Rillito was struggling and didn't seem long for this world, Zane was listening when his father made him what sounded like a good deal to buy the Trail's End. He knew his old man wanted to retire and move to Sedona with his girlfriend, the dental assistant he met when he was having a root canal. That was a couple of years after Zane's mom passed away, and the old man was tired of being alone. They went to the bank and each signed some papers and a note for fifty-grand, after which the banker shook Zane's hand.

"Congratulations," he said.

He wasn't entirely sure his old man hadn't screwed him on the deal until the liquor license came a couple of weeks later and had his name on it. He considered cleaning the place up and doing some redecorating but realized he didn't have any spare cash, so he and Loretta just touched up the paint and hung new curtains. For the first month or two he never saw a fresh face on any of the barstools. It seemed like Zane had inherited all his father's regular barflies, and the only newcomers were folks passing through Tucson on their way to someplace else. It took a while to get used to the way things were, but in a lot of ways the Trail's End regulars were like the people at the track - except nobody was betting on anything but football or basketball.

~~

Back when he worked at the track, Zane would see Rodney and Blinky on their bench under the tree, and if he stopped by, they'd take turns telling him lies. He once asked how they came to be friends.

"I was galloping an old mare for Buddy Delp over at Bowie," said Blinky. "Mister Delp, he was leading trainer most everyplace he went. He was a mailman before he trained horses. Learnt from his step-daddy Mister Archer. Trained the hair offa them claimers. Was before he got that Spectacular Bid when I was working for him, and mostly he had was claimers. But he put some over, always got you in the winner's circle, you know? Trained for the Meyerhoff brothers too, those guys used to drink Heineken beer all the time. They'd even drink it in the winner's circle, but they won so much nobody ever said they couldn't. One time the Mister Meyerhoff with the beard, he give me one of them green bottles, carried them with him in a little bag. Tasted mighty good, cold beer in the winner's circle."

"That's how you two met?" said Zane.

"Nossir, how we met was one morning at the track kitchen, break time. This one here," Blinky said, pointing at Rodney, "he bet his money the day before, and got beat a dirty nose. I recognized he wasn't a local, just another kid coming from Philadelphia, so he didn't know nobody and he looked hungry and I bought him breakfast."

At this Rodney raised an eyebrow.

"What he don't say, that it was his horse," said Rodney, "the one what beat me a nose for all my money."

Blinky laughed, stood, and slapped a knee.

"A dirty nose," Blinky said. "Saw that hang-dog face, looked like a little black puppy what just got whupped, looking in at me holding the mare in the winner's circle when they took our picture."

"We been friends ever since," said Rodney.

Rodney spent his mornings at the track from first light, armed with a stopwatch, trying to spot a horse that was sharp and ready to run. He kept meticulous notes, inscribed in a hand carefully nurtured by his schoolteacher mother. His signature would have made John Hancock proud.

For his efforts, Rodney received some compensation from the *Daily Racing Form*, known as The Bible to horseplayers. But the bulk of the income – on which he raised a daughter from his first marriage and three sons from the second – came mainly from betting on horses he identified as having more ability than the ones they were up against on race day.

Like most clockers, he was blessed with the patience to wait for a good price on a fast horse before he put up his cash. To keep a low profile, a major portion of those bets were made on Rodney's behalf by what is referred to around the track as an "egg" or a "sponsor." Those sponsors were basically losers who were eager to have Rodney's tips, hapless in the end because the track's cut of the betting pools would eat away at their feeble winnings. More often than not, they'd mortgage their house or sell their wife's diamond ring to fuel their plays, and she'd divorce them and they'd end up broke and alone. They could resist the devil himself, Rodney would say, but they couldn't pass on a hot tip on an even-money shot.

When the tip came in, they would brag to anyone who'd listen how smart they were to get the "inside information." But whenever the three-to-five shot finished up the track, they'd blame the jockey. Or the trainer. Or the weather. Or the track was too sloppy or too fast or the turf was too soft or too hard. But they never blamed the clocker, because if they did, he might not give them another one of those winning tips.

Rodney always managed to drive a new Plymouth sedan, usually a Grand Fury two-tone. He was partial to white and whatever might be the popular contrasting shade, but by the time he made Rillito way back when he was nursing a ten-year-old convertible, yellow and in need of a paint job. He said his vehicle upgrading plans had come to a halt when he realized none of his eastern eggs could bet into the tiny mutual pools at the bullrings without destroying their own odds. So he had to settle for making a living by taking modest stabs from his own retirement fund.

Blinky picked up his nickname one day at Pimlico during his stint as an apprentice jockey when he found himself under a pile of horses and riders at the quarter pole after a four-horse spill. He didn't lose the sight in his injured left eye, but the damage was enough to end his budding career and relegate him to the ranks of low-paid exercise riders who travelled from race meet to race meet. Eventually, he gravi-tated to the jockeys' room and took a job as a valet, a profession that must have suited him well. He did it for the next forty years.

Blinky said he never would have made a jockey anyway, that he knew right from the start that he wasn't going to make it when the trainer Tuffy Hacker lost Blinky's contract to Sunshine Calvert in a card game in the rec room at Monmouth Park, where the trainers would play racehorse rummy after their morning work. Unlike today, when they all have "the right to work," apprentice riders then had to be under contract to a stable. One day, when Tuffy mistook a club for a spade while pressing the last game, he didn't have enough cash to cover his loss, so Sunshine agreed to accept Blinky's contract to settle the debt.

Blinky swore that Tuffy did it on purpose just to get rid of him since only the day before he'd called him into the tack room and told him to listen up.

"Son, I been watching you gallop these race-horses for six months now, and either I'm a sorry ass excuse for a horse trainer or you've got less talent than the slowest nag in my barn. Better start thinking about another career," is what Tuffy said.

Finally came a time when, independent from each other, Rodney and Blinky bolted from the cold damp winters of the East to the warm, dry desert. They never said as much out loud, but they figured it was some kind of cosmic plan that pushed them together in southern Arizona, bouncing around the circuit of small tracks and eventually landing in Zane Rocco's lap, grateful for an audience to share tall tales of gamblers they had known.

"Worstest was Chalkie," said Blinky. "The man was a chalk-eating sonofagun. Thought if a horse wasn't favorite it must have something wrong with it."

They explained that "chalk" was what the gamblers called favorites, a throwback to the days when bookmakers displayed the odds on a blackboard and the horses who got the most action used up the most chalk since they had to keep erasing and changing their prices.

"Chalkie only cashed a bet on a longshot one time that I can recall," said Rodney. "It was a 52-to-1 shot he played the day he lost his glasses. He couldn't see for shit without them and thought the tote board said 5-to-2."

Blinky laughed so hard he halfway fell off the bench, caught himself, then jumped up and waved a finger in the air.

"Hah, that Chalkie," he said.

~~

Somehow, Rillito kept its doors open after Zane left the kitchen, but the track was barely running enough races to be remotely considered a going concern. Zane was hardly surprised one baking-hot afternoon to see Rodney and Blinky wander into the Trail's End.

"I figured it was only a matter of time before you guys would get bored enough to set up shop here," said Zane.

He poured them a couple of draughts.

"The old oak tree died and they had to cut it down," said Rodney. "Too hot to sit on that bench with no shade."

"You got any hard-boil eggs?" said Blinky.

"Can I get a bacon, egg, and cheese on a hard roll?" said Rodney.

Zane felt like he was right back at the Rillito kitchen. As they sat at the bar enjoying their impromptu lunch, both of them checked out the empty room and the exits to see if anyone might be within earshot.

"Awright, listen here son," said Rodney, just above a whisper. "We goin' to set up a score, an' we need your help. Kinda like fixin' a race, but nothing illegal."

Before Zane had a chance to wonder aloud at the fine legal point, Blinky picked up the plot.

"My cousin Cloney, back in Baltimore, he's got a three-year-old what run in the trials over the jumps down at Aiken last year, beat a good bunch by open lengths then chipped his knee," Blinky said. "Hasn't never run on the flat, but he's training back there like a good horse, in company with a colt what broke his maiden for thirty. Ain't nothin' around here can beat a horse what won a thirty maiden at Pimlico. Nothin'."

"But they only run one weekend a month here," Zane said, "and there's not enough money in the Rillito pools to get any kind of a price. If you bet more than a hundred the odds are shot."

"Exactly," said Blinky. "Except that Petey Diller, the little shit of a trainer what win a race here the other day, got himself an owner what thinks he's Diamond Jim. Man bets a couple thousand on his horses when they run at Rillito and makes them one-to-nine, but he don't care. Now he's been up to Phoenix and win one there at Turf Paradise, and compared to Rillito he thinks he's at Churchill Downs, so he can bet with both hands. I tole Petey I used to galloped back east and he axed did they use saddles back then. Smart little shit. Knows the name of the Unknown Soldier."

"What we do," said Rodney, "is bring this gelding from Maryland out here a couple of weeks after the new year, when he turns four. First time starter four-year-old with no form, West Virginia-bred by nobody out of nobody shows up in Arizona. His cousin gives us a bill of sale for two hundred in case anybody wants to know what he cost. Ain't nobody gonna give him a second look. We wait until Diller has one for a cheap maiden at Turf Paradise and we go in the same race."

"But he's got to show a workout before he runs," said Zane.

"Cole the track clocker sits in the grandstand at the wire," said Rodney, sketching on a cocktail napkin. "We'll fool him by working him slow and let a quarter-horse break off behind and pass him. Make him look like a bum. I'll be up there, chatting up ole Cole, so's he can't pay too much attention to how he's movin'."

"Besides, he gonna be being trained by some old fool like me, don't know what a saddle is," said Blinky.

Zane fiddled for time rearranging the bartop supply of olives and cherries.

"Well guys, I appreciate you telling me," he said, "but what do I have to do with this?"

"Here's the thing," said Rodney. "Diller's owner gonna build the pool, and what we need is somebody that we can trust to lay our bets. Mister Diamond Jim will maybe get the win pool up to twenty thousand while we bet a thousand on our boy a little at a time. We bet another thousand in Vegas and get twenty to one there, too. And then – bingo!"

"We get the whole pool," said Blinky.

The rest of the afternoon drifted by with more war stories before Rodney and Blinky said adios and melted into the twilight.

"What was that all about?" asked Loretta, emerging from the storeroom.

Zane gathered the fragments of eggshell and wiped the bar with a wet towel.

"My guys from Rillito want to break the bank at Vegas."

"So they haven't seen that lousy movie? Michael Caine, Morgan Freeman, and the old farts with the bank heist?"

"Something like that, I guess," said Zane. "One big score while they can still get it up."

"I think that ship might have sailed."

"They've got a hot horse and a great story to go with it."

"More likely you just got hustled for four drafts and two free lunches," Loretta said. "What's the name of this nag?"

Zane poured himself another Coors from the tap.

"Allshewrote," he said.

~~

Two weeks into the new year and the race meet was rolling at Turf Paradise. No races were run at Rillito but Blinky and a few other trainers were still stabled there galloping and breezing their horses every morning. Most of them would sit at the end of the grandstand in the bleacher seats and use binoculars to watch and some stood on the apron. Nobody missed much.

Rodney and Blinky leaned on the outside fence as Allshewrote approached. On board was Hidalgo the exercise boy who supplemented his social security as a quarter horse jockey. He must have weighed 130 pounds, wrung dry.

"How'd he go?" asked Blinky.

"Put me on him boss, I'll ride him," said Hidalgo. "Got a little hitch in his gitalong though."

Rodney and Blinky spoke as one.

"He got a what?" they said.

"Hits the ground funny right back there," said Hidalgo, nodding toward the horse's rear end as they approached the rail gap.

"You go cool him out," said Blinky to Rodney. "I gotta call my cousin."

Rodney was giving Allshewrote a bath by the time Blinky got back to the barn.

"What he say?" asked Rodney.

"Say he's sound as a bell of brass, but he goes funny behind," Blinky said. "His momma went the same way, he says. Say she always looked like she was gonna fall down sometimes, but still ran like a scalded cat. How'd he cool out?"

"Hardly a deep breath and his ankles an' knees are cold and tight. I jogged him on the road and he never so much as nodded a wink."

"So maybe Cloney's right?" said Blinky.

"Horse says he is," said Rodney. "Let's put him on the van."

An hour later the two old men took their usual spot at the end of the bar. Zane dumped a bucket of ice over an assortment of beer bottles in the trough.

"You know what I heard?" said Rodney.

"Not yet," said Blinky.

"Heard Honey Buns is gone to meet her maker."

"Honey Buns? From the track kitchen, what was cashier? Cute blonde? With the big – "

"Yep," said Rodney.

"Dang," said Blinky. "First Little Joe, then Rocky and Peaches, all in a row, and now that little Honey Buns. Dang."

"And Fats and Sonny before them," said Rodney. "Don't forget them."

"I'm beginning to think you two make a game of reminding each other who's gone," said Zane.

"No," said Rodney. "Just keeping track."

Blinky took a long look into his half empty glass, shook his head and said, "Waiting for my turn."

At which point the Trail's End front door swung open and Jaime, the kid from the racing office, dropped an overnight sheet on the bar with entries for the weekend card at Turf Paradise. Rodney gave the sheet a look and handed it to Blinky.

"Number ten of ten," said Rodney.

"That's good," said Blinky. "Don't have to stand in the gate and wait while the other horses load. He can go to the front and not look back. Little Petey Diller and his Diamond Jim got the rail. They'll be bettin' with both hands on that colt they finished second with last time for twenty thousand, dropping him in for eight and thinking they geniuses. You think this is gonna work?"

"Between you, Rodney, and Hidalgo, that's about two hundred years of experience," Zane said. "That ought to count for something."

~~

Turf Paradise in northwest Phoenix is, in fact, a lot like a big-time track compared to Rillito, but Rodney, Blinky, Zane and Loretta were not interested in sightseeing. They split up as the race approached, with Zane and Loretta spreading around their bets while the guys prepared Allshewrote for battle.

"Bet twenty to win at the odd numbered windows from left to right and I'll do the evens," said Zane.

"Then we'll change hats and put glasses on, and you do the evens and I'll do the odds.

"This is exciting," said Loretta, touching her chest. "I'm getting a little warm, right here."

"Maybe we should do twenty-five a bet," said Zane, missing the point. As he handed her the cash she winked and fingered the red strap of her bra to make certain he knew she wasn't talking about the weather. He told her they'd meet at the ice cream stand.

Zane ordered two mint chocolate chip cones and nodded nervously toward the lights flashing five minutes to post. He showed Loretta the inside of the manila envelope he'd been toting with the cash. Empty. She winked again and grazed her hand across his crotch.

"Maybe we should just check into that motel across the street," she said. "Save driving home that late."

"Nah, we'll cash and then blow town," Zane said before thinking.

She was nuzzling close enough now that he got the scent of her soap.

"Yeah, we should stay," he said. "Yeah."

After saddling Allshewrote and giving a leg up to Hidalgo, Rodney and Blinky mixed with the grandstand crowd and made their way to the stairwell at the end of the building across from the sixteenth pole.

Rodney kept his binoculars locked on Allshewrote as the horses and ponies closed in on the starting gate. He let out a gasp.

"Oh, momma, we're screwed," Rodney groaned.

"What, what?" said Blinky.

"Sweet Jesus."

"Jesus what?" said Blinky.

"A horse flipped. They going to scratch him," said Rodney. "I think he landed on his back. They have to."

"I ain't seeing what you say," said Blinky, "but that sure looks like us back of the gate, standing like a gentleman."

"I'm not talking about our horse. Talkin' bout Diller's!"

"Oh!" said Blinky, staring into the distance. "Oh no."

Inside the grandstand, beneath a bank of TV monitors, Loretta was first to notice the numbers on the tote board go nuts as the horses made their final approach to the starting gate.

"Why are we all of a sudden the favorite?" she asked. "Three-to-five? We were 20-to-1 a minute ago."

"Shit," Zane said, just as the voice of the public address announcer began to echo through the building.

"Ladies and gentlemen, may I have your attention please ..."

"They scratched the favorite," said Zane. "And all Diamond Jim's money went away in refunds. The two-grand we bet is half the pool now."

"So that's it?" she said. "No forty thousand?"

"We'll be lucky to make a thousand. And it's too late now to cancel the bets."

~~

Coming back from the race, Hidalgo threw kisses to the crowd and waved his whip at the stewards, signaling that Allshewrote was home safe and sound as they entered the winner's circle. Zane and Loretta flanked Rodney as Blinky gave the horse and rider a short turn and stood them straight for the track photographer.

"Smile," said the photographer. "You guys look like somebody just died."

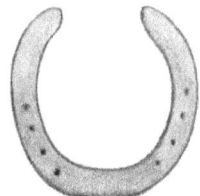

HEAD CASE

"Gimmie a Maker's, neat. And a water, no ice," said the stranger.

I poured him a good dose and slid it across the bar and he downed it before I filled his water. He stared at the empty glass as if it were a cellphone and he was a lovestruck teenager reading a text from his girl. He put the glass down gently and slid it toward me.

"Steve," he said, extending his hand. "Steve Tramont."

"Jack," I said, administering a firm grip. He had soft hands, the kind that had never held a shovel or a saw.

"You'd be the proprietor of this establishment, would you?"

"That's me," I said.

He pointed at the winner's circle pictures on the walls.

"Horse racing guy is my guess."

"Good guess."

"Love the ponies," he said.

I nodded agreement and pointed toward the wall with the rack of pool cues. We shared a moment's contemplation of one of my prized possessions, a black and white photo hanging there from the forties immortalizing a quarter horse mare named Shue Fly winning by a nose at Rillito Park, our local track. I proffered today's copy of a *Daily Racing Form* and he declined.

"On the wagon," he said. "But I still love the sport."

He pushed the empty glass for a refill.

"I was big in the game for a while," he said. "Had a bunch of good ones out at Santa Anita. Dark Jester, Occlusion, Nose Tweaker – "

"I heard of them, pretty good bunch," I said. "What was it, Crystal Ball Stable? White silks with a red cap? That was you?"

He nodded, a broad smile crossing his face.

"I made a winter book bet on Dark Jester for the Derby right after he broke his maiden," I said. "Got 100-to-1 on twenty bucks at Caesars World. What ever happened to him?"

"Stands at stud in Oklahoma," he said. "They breed him mainly to quarter horse mares for five hundred a pop. Sonofagun could fly for a half-mile but couldn't get a step over five-eighths."

His glass came my way again and I gave him another generous pour. Years at this profession told me here was another guy who had a story to tell and I was going to hear it, which was okay by me. Most of the tales I sit through are either bemoaning a heartbreak or political rants. At least this one was about the racetrack.

"I was selling used cars over in Cerritos at the Auto Mall. Nobody sold more than me," he said. "One night some of the guys took me to Los Alamitos and I hit the late double. Bet my wife's birthday, seven and seven, and got back $322 for my two bucks. That was it.

"I started to head to the track every day for the last few races, whatever track was open – Hollywood, Santa Anita, Los Al, Pomona," he said. "Went there every day for twelve years and got into it pretty heavy. I don't mean the bets, just the game. I was always a ten and twenty-buck punter most of the time, once in a while fifty to win and place, but I was serious about it, you know? Student of the form, as they say.

"Anyway, I liked to stand by the rail when the jocks came back and give them an earful when they got beat. You gotta blame somebody, right? That was a big part of the fun to me, screaming at the little pricks when they'd lose a bet for me. At least I got my money's worth blowing off some steam in their direction."

I nodded like I always do when the storytellers get to this point, humoring them until they need another drink. But soon he had my full attention.

"I used to like that Happy Hour they had at the Houston's over on Arroyo Parkway," he said. "One night I stopped there on my way home from Santa Anita and a useless jockey named Smilin' Jack Suarez had just cost me a two-thousand-dollar tri in the last race, posing for his picture when they came to the wire and getting himself nipped for the win by some bug boy on a 20-to-1 shot. I'd already had a couple of pops and I was pretty loosened up when I called him a no-ridin' little pinhead and he took umbrage. You never think it's going to be much of a fight, you against a guy you outweigh by eighty pounds."

I poured him another.

"The little fucker caught me with an uppercut, and it took the best oral surgeon in Pasadena three hours to wire my jaw," he said. "I wouldn't be too sure he didn't have a roll of dimes in his fist. About a week later I started to hear the voices."

"Voices," I heard myself echo.

"Actually, just one," he said. "Trevor Denman."

"The announcer?" I said and he nodded.

"At first I thought I was dreaming – daydreaming like when you get a song stuck in your head, until it happened when I was leaving the carwash on Walnut. I had an old Bimmer that I treated like a lady. I got her washed once a week, waxed every month. I was pulling out onto Sierra Madre Boulevard when I hear Trevor saying 'Doubleton is drawing clear by five. They'd need to sprout wings to catch him!'

"I'd been reading the *Racing Form* while the car was getting washed and I knew Doubleton was in the fifth race. Only it was the next day," he said. "He was in the next day, not *that* day. *That* day was a Tuesday and there weren't any races. I thought I was going nuts."

A gorilla could have walked in the front door and I wouldn't have taken my eyes off the guy.

"Next day I go the Great Race Place and sit in my usual spot," he said. "Grandstand side, second floor, where they got those high-top tables. I like to spread my *Form* out on them and there's never anybody around there anyway. The odds board is saying that Doubleton is 33-to-1. So I go to the window and bet fifty on him and just watch it on the TV over the bar. He runs out of the picture, he's so far in front. Pays $67.40 and I win seventeen hundred. Up to then the most I ever won was three-four hundred."

It was a pretty good story he was spinning, so I poured him another pop and hoped he wouldn't get too drunk before he got to the end.

"I start betting as much as I can without affecting the odds too much, every time I hear the voice," he said. "And it ain't wrong. Ever.

"I hear it once or twice a week and never could figure out why, if it was the weather or the wind direction or the humidity. Might happen anytime, anyplace. Might be a favorite, even-money with Pincay or some 20-to-1 shot with Larry Gilligan, nothing you could figure out. One day I was getting my hair cut at that little dive barbershop under the YMCA in Pasadena and I heard him call a horse a winner by a nose. Next afternoon I bet a thousand on it and almost had a heart attack with the photo, it was that close. But the sonofabitch won."

I poured myself a shot from the same bottle.

"Took down half a million over the next six months," he said. "And kept it to myself. You coulda stood right next to me and the only way you'd have known I won was if you took my blood pressure. Even my old lady didn't know, I was so slick about it, throwing her a couple hundred when I scored big and telling her I lost the other days.

"I began to think maybe I should be a horse owner, quit hanging out with the bunch of losers in the cheap seats and become one of those guys in the paddock talking to the trainers and the jockeys. Those guys they're interviewing after the race. And I was, real quick. Bought one from Canani for twenty grand that was easily worth ten and told him to run it for sixty-five hundred and of course it won. Pretty soon I had a dozen hides carrying my silks and my own spot in the owner's lot with the swells. Kurt Hoover interviewed me on TV and asked me 'what was my biggest thrill in horseracing.' I told him it was knowing who was going to win before the race. With a straight face I said that, and he didn't know what to say."

I wasn't sure, but there might have been a tear in the corner of his eye.

"I was God," he said. "*God at the racetrack.*"

Probably at that point not a good idea, but I had to ask.

"So what brings you to Tucson?"

He put down the bourbon and looked me straight in the eye. He had a square jaw, with a few tiny scars on one check, steel-grey hair slicked back, and pale blue eyes that were almost white. It was a desperate stare and slightly unnerving, like somebody trying to look into your soul, or leave theirs.

"My balance in the horseman's account was seven figures and besides the bunch I had with

Canani, I had another dozen with Mel Stute," he said. "I told my mother I was on top of the world, just like Cagney in 'White Heat.'"

He could see I was no expert on vintage flicks.

"'Made it, ma! Top of the world!' is what Cagney said."

"Yeah, right," I said, my memory jogged. "And then he was blown sky high."

He gave me a look that said, "No kidding."

"We were 12-to-1 in the feature one day at Santa Anita," he said, "and I was following my horse from the saddling area to the paddock. I had heard Trevor the day before, calling my horse a winner, so I knew I was a cinch and feeling like a genius. I made some smart-ass comment to Stute about a blonde on the rail with legs up to here, and when I turned the horse kicked out and caught me flush. I woke up in the ER and they were wiring my jaw again."

"Let me guess," I said. "No more Trevor."

"No more voices and no more winners," he said. "I went through my whole bankroll faster than a fat guy can finish a quart of Baskin Robbins butter pecan. Scraped up enough to come out here and make a fresh start."

"Man oh man," I said, shaking my head. "With horses?"

"Nah, I'm done with the ponies. Easy come, easy go," he said, slapping a twenty on the bar. "I just opened a used car lot over on Speedway. Calling it Miracle Motors. *'Bad credit. No credit? Legally dead? C'mon in!'*"

I laughed.

"Keep the change," he said with a wink as he headed for the door. "And be careful who you listen to."

POCKETS

The day after Carl Willson graduated from St. Rose of Lima high school, a couple of blocks from Belmar Beach, he went fishing off the Twelfth Avenue jetty. That's where he caught the 33-pound striper about three years before, on his thirteenth birthday. He caught a few around 20 pounds over the years, but the 33-pounder was the one they still talked about at the firehouse where his father was on the volunteer squad.

A lot of the firemen fished and they had a scale there, so that was where Carl took his prize catch. The chief snapped a Polaroid that was still thumbtacked to the wall years later. Carl was proud of that fish and happy to take it home and clean it, cutting enough steaks for the family to enjoy for the rest of the summer. But when he read in *Field and Stream* that the fish was probably the same age as he was, he thought about that for a while and began to cry. After that, he released everything he caught.

Carl didn't catch anything the day after his graduation, and when he stopped at the firehouse afterwards, they told him to get home right away, because his mother had been looking for him.

Carl's mother made him sit down on the brown corduroy couch in the living room and told him that his father had been up on a ladder in front of the garage trying to fix the spotlight when he touched his screwdriver to a live wire. They weren't sure right away if it was the shock that killed him, or falling off the ladder, but Carl didn't hear much of anything his mother said after she said your Daddy's dead.

Carl had no brothers or sisters, so for the next six months it was just him and his mom living there in the little white house with the green shutters, square in the middle of town. It was Christmas when she decided to take a handful of barbiturates along with the bottle of vodka that had become a staple of her daily diet.

His mother's brother Leon was a dour cynic of fifty-seven who lived by himself in a one-bedroom apartment above the Woolworths on Main Street in Asbury Park. Uncle Leon told Carl they would have to sell the house and there wouldn't be much money left after the funeral expenses and paying off the mortgage and his mom's credit cards. He said Carl could sleep on his back porch, but he'd have to get a job and pay some rent if he wanted to stick around. The porch was screened in, but no good when the weather was cold. As Leon was a single man who worked as a conductor on the Jersey Central line, he didn't care much for looking after a teenager, and by that spring Carl was fending for himself.

Carl had been to the races at Monmouth Park a few times with his old man and Mr. Giannelli, one of his teachers from St. Rose, who had a summer job there as a hot walker. He told Carl that all you do is walk the horses around for about half an hour after they come back from their exercise, and the only thing you need to know, really, is how to turn left and how to tell time.

Mr. Giannelli first took Carl to the track one morning at daybreak, but after that Carl drove himself in his mother's Chevy Nova even though he didn't have a driver's license yet. He thought it was interesting, how they would give you a license to work at the track when you were sixteen, but you had to be seventeen to get a driver's license.

The trainer that gave Carl his job told him he could live at the barn, which sounded a lot better to Carl than camping out on Uncle Leon's porch. He packed the Nova with his clothes, his fishing tackle and a couple of books and never saw his uncle again.

~~

For the three months the track was open that first summer, Carl shared a 12-by-12 tack room with a groom everyone called Sherman. No first name, just Sherman. They each had a mattress on a wire framed cot, a footlocker for possessions, and a little cabinet with one drawer and a bedside lamp. The trunk of the Nova served as Carl's storage room, and when that became too crowded he began to fill the back seat. He parked the car in the back at the far end of the barn and only moved it once a week when the feed truck came and they needed to unload the hay and straw.

The first week he was there, the assistant trainer told him their best horse was going to have a workout and he should go to the starter's office and get the key to the quarter pole. A few days later one of the grooms told him one of his horses had a stuffy nose and he needed Carl to go to the head veterinarian and bring back a bucket of steam. Carl was embarrassed when he realized he'd been had, but Sherman just smiled and shook his head, told him not to mind their jokes, they did the same to all rookies.

Carl figured Sherman might be old enough to be his grandfather. He was a man of few words, carrying a couple of hundred pounds on a five foot-four frame and sporting a prominent nose he'd inherited from his Greek mother. Duct tape held his horn-rimmed glasses together. Carl tried to start a conversation a few times but gave up when he couldn't get Sherman to volunteer more than a yes or a no. The only time the old man would say anything much was on Saturday night, after he'd had a few pops from the fifth of whiskey someone would drop off after the last race.

"Ain't left the stable area of a racetrack in thirty years," Sherman said.

With only that to go on, Carl was left to piece together Sherman's story for himself. He knew Sherman ate his breakfast, lunch, and dinner at the track kitchen and an occasional hot dog and a beer in the grandstand.

"Where are you from?" asked Carl.

"Born'n Chicago. Out by Arlington Park," said Sherman.

"Ever go home?"

He just shook his head.

"Florida for the winter," said Sherman.

Carl decided he would keep walking horses, moving on wherever the stable went when the season ended. Sherman told him that after Labor Day they would head to Atlantic City for six weeks, then Garden State Park for another six before the season ended and all the stables would scatter, some to

Florida or New Orleans, some to farms for the winter, then in the spring back to Monmouth Park, which Carl had come to think of as home.

It sounded crazy, but it suited Carl, and he settled into the life. He had nothing else going on, and the stall man at Monmouth let him leave his car in an empty equipment shed while he traveled in the van with Sherman and the horses.

The horses were mostly kind, and he liked to talk to them as they cooled out during the thirty or forty minutes it took them to unwind before their groom gave them a bath and put them back in their stall. When all the horses were put away, Carl would sweep the blacktop outside the barn and rake the shed row in a neat herringbone pattern Sherman taught him before he went to the tack room and read for an hour or so before heading to the kitchen for lunch.

Sometimes around midday Carl would hold a horse for the blacksmith or the vet or help the grooms wash bandages, but most days he liked to wander the stable area, scavenging for odds and ends that others had lost or discarded. He found a pair of binoculars in a trash can - one side worked fine if he closed his other eye - and he found he could follow the races just fine from one of the clocker's stands Sherman told him about.

In the evening when no one was around he liked to visit the horses he liked best, telling them about his day or something he'd learned. He brought sugar cubes from the track kitchen and gave them to the horses as a reward if they acted like they understood what he was talking about. Some would stick out their tongue, others would nod or shake their head. The sugar cubes were free but he'd only take a few at a time because he didn't want anyone to think he was stealing.

In truth, Carl had become an enthusiastic collector of backstretch souvenirs. One day he took two of the magazines someone had left on the table with the napkins, mustard, and ketchup. He would grab discarded condition books scattered around the racing office and track kitchen once they were no longer of their brief use. Grooms used the pages of the little booklets anyway to seal the mud they packed in horses' feet to reduce inflammation. Carl wasn't a groom and didn't pack any feet, but he was fascinated by the abundance of so many free things that could impart any kind of racetrack information.

At the end of each day, the pockets of his green cargo pants and jacket would be filled with brochures for stud farms, maps, religious tracts, horse sale catalogs, track programs and coupons, as well as matchbooks, pencils, and pens. Sherman took umbrage at having their tack room turned into a storage facility, so Carl would transfer his inventory to the Nova, and before long there was barely enough room to get behind the wheel.

~~

Carl finished the last of his scrambled eggs, pushing them on his fork with a crust of rye toast, and washed them down with some of the nasty track kitchen coffee that was always too hot to drink until you'd already finished your breakfast. He looked up occasionally at the TV overhead to see if Let's Make A Deal was on yet. It was his favorite.

He watched Mr. Arbogast, the track announcer, hand the cashier a hundred-dollar bill and pocket his change, pick up the tray with his coffee and a bagel and cream cheese and a *Daily Racing Form* and move on to the same table against the wall where he always ate, always by himself. Mr. Arbogast liked to sit with his back to the wall so he could spot anyone coming his way and wave them off if he was too engrossed in his homework, which was memorizing the jockeys' silks for that day's racing. Carl saw him do the same thing every day and wondered what he did with the rest of his time. Did he have a family, a wife and kids or live alone? If maybe he had a dog or a cat? He wondered if Mr. Arbogast's parents were living, or if he too were an orphan.

Mounted on the wall behind where Mr. Arbogast sat was a huge, sepia-tinted aerial photo of the track probably taken in the 1950s, showing its parking lot filled to capacity back when the sport was in its heyday. It seemed an appropriate backdrop for the announcer, who was somewhat of an anachronism himself. Mr. Arbogast's sallow, pock-marked complexion and few extra pounds made him look older than he really was, but he dressed the part. Carl had never seen Mr. Arbogast without a suit and tie, his polished brown and white spectators, and a straw hat – sometimes a pork pie and other times a boater. Carl imagined Mr. Arbogast watched a lot of old movies and liked the way those men dressed back in the day, particularly at the racetrack.

Carl pictured himself in Mr. Arbogast's booth, high atop the grandstand gazing down at the finish line. He imagined using his voice the way Mr. Arbogast did, like a musical instrument, increasing its volume and quickening to a crescendo, building excitement as the horses approached the finish line.

He loved the way Mr. Arbogast would always call the winner, never hedging like the announcers who would exclaim "too close to call!" or "photo finish!" as if everyone watching didn't already know that it was close. The man had no fear of making a mistake, and Carl took extra pleasure in remembering the time he heard Mr. Arbogast call a dead heat.

Although they'd never exchanged a single word, Carl liked to imagine they were best friends, that Mr. Arbogast would come by the tack room at the end of the barn where he had lived for the past three years. He wondered if Mr. Arbogast liked to fish, so maybe sometime they would go buy some mossbunkers for bait and fish together from one of the jetties.

Beyond such idle imaginings, Carl had no aspirations for a higher racetrack calling. He was too tall and too heavy to be a jockey. The job demanded of the grooms seemed like a lot of hard work. As for the trainer, that was way too much responsibility. He was okay with walking horses. It didn't pay much, but he had a place to sleep and more than enough money for food.

~~

They were in line, Mr. Arbogast waiting for his daily bagel, Carl for his eggs.

"Mr. Pockets," said Mr. Arbogast. His tie was loosened and he had a dab of talcum powder on his throat where he'd cut himself shaving.

Carl stared at him. It didn't register right away that the announcer was actually speaking to him.

Mr. Arbogast indicated the bulging pockets of Carl's cargo pants.

Carl smiled, wondering why anyone would care about his pockets, full or otherwise. But he was pleased just to be acknowledged, especially by Mr. Arbogast. He stepped aside to let a groom pass.

"Do you have a dog?" Carl asked.

"No," said Mr. Arbogast. "But we used to have one when I was a kid, back in Cincinnati. A mutt named Skippy."

"I like dogs," said Carl.

"I have enough trouble, just taking care of myself," said Mr. Arbogast.

"Do you have parents?"

"Sure, but they both passed away," said Mr. Arbogast. "My father before I was ten and mother just last year. You?"

Carl shook his head.

"I think if I had a dog, I'd have a Labrador," said Carl. "A chocolate Lab. You have to brush them a lot because they shed so much. But I wouldn't mind."

"I considered getting a cat," said Mr. Arbogast, "but my girlfriend was allergic. My ex-girlfriend."

A pair of exercise girls smiled at Mr. Arbogast and said hi as they pushed their trays past.

"Cats are okay too," said Carl. "But I'd have a dog."

"You a groom?" asked Mr. Arbogast.

"Nah, I'm just a hotwalker."

"I don't mind giving them a carrot, but otherwise they scare me to death, they're so big," said Mr. Arbogast. "Much safer at a distance, through these."

He tugged on the leather strap over his shoulder, attached to his ever-present binocular case.

"Most of them are really nice," said Carl. "Sally and Emma mainly, they're the nicest. You should come by the barn and see them. They won't hurt you."

Mr. Arbogast retrieved his bagel from the counter.

"Sure, maybe," he said. "See you around Mr. Pockets."

~~

Milo Arbogast was descending alone in the press box elevator. At the end of a racing day he liked to wait until everyone else had left before making his exit. He would cross by the empty paddock on his way to the parking lot, wading through the litter of programs and losing mutuel tickets left behind by the fans who had filled the track.

He drove out the back gate of the track and across the railroad tracks through the far end of the stable area, passing a lone security guard who waved a perfunctory goodbye.

Stopping by the poultry farm in Long Branch on his way home, Milo picked up a rotisserie chicken.

He was disappointed that the blonde girl who usually took his order wasn't there. He had begun to think she might like him, the way she always wrapped his chicken, neat and tidy, and gave him a big smile when she handed him his change. He considered asking her if she wanted to meet him at the Italian Ice place down by the beach and thought maybe they could take a walk to the park a couple of blocks away. He wondered about her name, where she lived, if she had a dog. He wondered if she might like him if he had a puppy.

As he climbed the stairs to his apartment on the second floor, Milo could smell the aromas wafting from the Italian restaurant below. He had lived alone there for the past ten years starting when his mother went in the nursing home, and he never cooked for himself other than boiling a couple of hot dogs and heating some baked beans or scrambling some eggs. He pondered for a moment if maybe he should opt for a plate of pasta and decided to wait until Saturday to treat himself to a carbonara.

From the front balcony he could see the Atlantic Ocean, flat from an onshore breeze that was keeping the temperature toasty. He set a placemat at the small round patio table before fetching a beer to go with his chicken.

The shoreline view was unobstructed for a quarter mile in both directions. Across Ocean Avenue there was an old man walking an old dog, taking their time and enjoying the evening. When he finished dinner, Milo turned on the television and cleared the coffee table to make room for his program from the day's races so he could go over the results. He wondered again if maybe he should have a dog. Yeah, I should do that, he thought, someone to talk to. The idea made him smile.

~~

Carl put the paper sack containing his dinner on the windowsill of the horsemen's lounge while he perused the bulletin board, a collection of notes and advertisements and business cards. There were ads to sell horses and tack, to board horses, or buy them or ship them. Carl noticed a photo of a box full of Australian shepherd puppies and imagined himself calling the number and the lady that answered telling him she only had one left and he should hurry over if he wanted it, and him saying he would call her back.

Carl walked the main road to the track kitchen, then the back road to the barn, past the track's firehouse. Some evenings when it reminded him of his father he might stop at the bench outside the firehouse and eat his dinner from a brown paper bag, maybe a sandwich or a burrito, or a cup of soup and a biscuit.

Other nights he set a folding chair outside the door of his room so he could sit and eat his fried chicken while watching the horses' heads poked outside their stall doors. He emptied his pockets of the day's scavenging: a dozen condition books, two handfuls of prayer books from the track chaplain's office, a broken yo-yo, some mustard and ketchup packets from the kitchen, several bottlecaps, and a bunch of new, unsharpened pencils from the horsemen's lounge.

Carl popped the top on a can of root beer and washed down the last of the chicken before retrieving a handful of red and white peppermints from his room, being careful not to disturb the sleeping Sherman. By the time he got to the first horse and unwrapped the peppermint, all the rest along the row had their heads out in anticipation. He went to the next stall, fed the horse his candy, and smiled.

BET ON RED

"Imagine now you are floating on a raft in the blue-green water of the Caribbean. The water is crystal clear. So clear you can see right to the bottom, to the sand and the coral reef below."

The therapist had a soft, hypnotic tone.

"The air is warm. A light breeze caresses your skin. You are floating on a raft, and the water is warm as your legs and arms dangle over the side of the raft. The air smells sweet and salty."

Dev could feel his chest rising and settling, his eyes rolling back.

"Now, Dev, place your hand on your chest. Press with your thumb, then your index finger, then the second, the third and your little finger. Whenever you want to get back to this place, this peaceful floating on a warm sea, just hold your hand there and press your fingers."

Dev was there, almost floating, when her phone dinged to indicate time was up and the session had ended.

"Okay, we'll get into your breathing next time," she said.

He sat up and shook his head. She was close enough to smell her scent. It wasn't tropical, and he wasn't on a raft.

~~

Rube had dark, wavy hair, cold blue eyes and gentle hands, which were the first things women noticed. And it came to him naturally, beginning with the day his high school history teacher broke him in at her beach cabana. He was the quarterback on the football team and never had to do more than nod at any girl to get whatever he wanted – cheerleaders, waitresses, even co-eds at Santa Monica Community College.

And so it went, until he turned thirty and met Paula by chance at a seaside amusement park, playing miniature golf with mutual friends. They ended up next to each other in the concession line, and she snubbed him when he tried to turn on the charm. It took a week for him to find out who she was and get her phone number from his friend Barry. She and Barry had gone out a few times, but Barry was a player just like Rube and never stayed with anyone for very long.

But Paula was different, and he never looked at another woman in the same way again. When they were on their second date, he told her his ideas about opening a surf shop and how he was working on his business plan and asked her to marry him, all pretty much in one breath. She said let's wait a while and see how things work out.

Paula was getting tired of her job at the DMV, sitting behind a counter and listening to idiots try to explain why they forgot to bring two valid forms of identification to get a driver's license along with all the versions of why she should take their word that they are who they say they are. Not potential terrorists, just garden variety morons.

At a rate of only one course per semester at Loyola, it was going to be a decade before she'd earn a law degree, but if that was what it was going to take, so be it. In the meantime, she'd had about enough of the cramped apartment two blocks from the beach that she and Rube rented a year and a half ago when they decided to move in together. She could hardly remember the last time she spent time on the sand. When she did she'd get a sunburn, or a rash from the sunscreen, for her sin of being a brown-eyed redhead. But it was warm most of the time, and since she grew up in Idaho she didn't care if she ever saw snow again.

Rube, on the other hand, seemed content to wait tables three nights a week at the country club. He thought earning too much money might be a negative, just more taxes to pay. So much for his business plan. "You make too much money," he'd say, "people just kidnap your kids." If he and his friends spent as much time working as they did gambling and hustling, she thought, they'd all be millionaires.

And the sonofabitch could get a tan sitting next to a sixty-watt lightbulb. She wondered what she saw in him, other than the tall, good looks and the pale blue eyes that used to give her a chill. He was still tall.

~~

Walking into the paddock before the fifth race at Santa Anita, Dev figured it was the sight of the red-headed kid with his father reading a program on the paddock rail that made him flash back to his mother's ham and cheese sandwiches and how she had clapped her hands and squealed when he and his dad got home from the first time they went to the horse races and his dad tossed his $245 in winnings on the kitchen table.

He slapped his whip on the side of his boot as he approached the trainer and the owner of the horse he was about to ride.

"We're good today, Dev," said the trainer, as the owner nodded like a bobblehead.

"You're down for five hundred on the nose," said the bobblehead.

"Go to the front and improve your position," said the trainer, which was the same thing the trainer of the horse in the previous race had said. Dev wondered if every trainer was going to use that line today.

"You got it, boss," said Dev, adding a wink and a thumbs up to the tall blonde wife of the bobblehead owner. She blushed, but her husband was preoccupied and wouldn't suspect anyway that she wanted desperately to screw their jockey and was doing everything possible to make it happen.

After the last race of the day, Dev finished dressing and arranged the contents of his cubicle shelf like he did each day before he left the jockeys' room. Shaving cream and razor on the right. Deodorant, shampoo, conditioner, moisturizer, Vaseline, and Chapstick on the left. Rubber bands on the second shelf within handy reach. Two pair of clean underwear, two sleeveless t-shirts, two pair of socks, and his whips crossed on the bottom shelf.

The Saint Christopher medal that his mother gave him hung from a hook. He hadn't been in church since high school, back when he decided that the stories the nuns were telling him weren't much different than the fairy tales his grandmother read to him before bed. But after he'd had a few spills and survived, he figured it was better to cover all the bases, just in case.

He took five bills from the wad of hundreds out of the envelope the bobblehead owner had sent to the jockey's room after the race, then reconsidered, put three back, and gave the other two to his valet.

"Good day today, Johnny," he said. "Get yourself a bottle of Patron."

"Gracias," said the valet, tucking them in his shirt pocket. "College fund."

~~

Paula turned Rube's favorite jeans inside out before tossing them in the wash. It was a trick her mother had taught her to keep from wearing out the denim. Rube said he had worn the jeans to a Paul McCartney concert at Staples Center in 2005, and they still looked pretty good.

As she checked the pockets, a few slips of paper fell to the floor. She picked them up - three betting tickets from the last race at Santa Anita, a couple of Powerball tabs, and a matchbook cover with a phone number along with the message "See you later!" and a doodled smiley face.

It wasn't Rube's lousy handwriting, and he didn't smoke.

Paula shoved the suspicious flotsam into her shorts and continued her chores - all the chores, in fact, after a full shift at the DMV. She was in the bedroom folding Rube's clothes as the setting sun had begun to filter through the apartment's front blinds when she heard the front door open and Rube toss his keys on the table.

"Hey," he said as draped his jacket on a dining table chair.

"Hey," she replied coming into the room.

She asked how his Friday went, as if he could have had a tough one shooting baskets with his friends at the beachfront park in Venice and hanging out afterwards with Barry at Chez Jay, drinking beers and eating the free peanuts.

"Okay," he said and went in the bedroom.

A man of few words, she thought.

"I made fried chicken for dinner," she said. "Are you going to shower?"

"Did you wash my jeans?" he said.

"Yeah, in the dryer."

She heard him open the dryer door. Sure, have yourself a look, she thought.

"Yeah, okay," he said.

"Twenty minutes."

"Okay. I'm going to shower."

She heard the water running.

"Hey, Paula?" he said. She made him call again. "Paula?"

"What, hon'?" she said.

"Didn't find any tickets around here, did you? From the track and a couple of lottery tickets? I might have left them in my jeans."

"Nope," she said. The shower door closed.

Asshole, she thought. As she began to mash the potatoes the visions returned. She saw his face, twisted in terror, the fork with which he shoveled the potatoes still in his hand as he gasped for air. He grabbed at his throat and tore open his black work shirt from the club. *How long it would take for the rat poison to finish the job*, she wondered, *and what would it look like as he convulsed on the floor.* The vision ended, unresolved, and once again she wished she wouldn't have such intrusive images straight out of a Hitchcock movie.

"Beer?" he asked, cracking a can of Coors and putting it at his place at the table.

"No thanks, hon'," she said.

She put the platter of fried chicken in front of him between the creamed spinach and the mashed potatoes and turned back to finish mixing chives in the sour cream.

"Find your tickets?" she said.

"Nah, they were Barry's anyway," he said. "And nobody hit the Powerball. Heard it on the news. It's up to three hundred million."

"Three hundred forty," she said. "That's worth winning. I'd give a million to everybody I know. Even the kid that mows the lawn. Just to see what they all do with it."

"All those people who win the big ones go crazy," he said. "They end up broke anyway. I'd hire my own accountant and pay myself a salary, write it off. I'd put everything into a trust, just live off the investments."

"Kind of like you do now, those investments at the track? And the casino."

"Yeah," he said. "I should invest in dolls, like you."

She filled her glass with ice water and took her place across from him at the table. The flat was small and cramped like most of the apartments near Santa Monica beach, with one bedroom and one bath and a rectangular space that served as a living and dining room that looked out a sliding glass door onto a dinky patch of grass with a board fence that separated it from an identical apartment next door.

"I won't be able to go to your mom's tomorrow," he said. "I have to go to the track again with Barry. His friend has a tip."

"Same friend that had the last tip?" she said. "Back at Hollywood Park? The one that's still running?"

"Naw, this is different. Barry says he met some woman at the car lot buying an almost new Jaguar for cash. Married to a jockey over at Santa Anita. They hit it off and Barry says there's one going tomorrow she says is a cinch."

"Barry ever hit it off with anyone who's not married?" she said.

Rube laughed and fetched a bottle of hot sauce from the fridge.

"Did you pay the rent?" she said.

"I'll pay it on Monday. I think that's when it's due."

He knows damn well when it's due, she thought. *And he knows damn well what happened last time he had a hot tip and I had to borrow money from my mother to make the rent.*

"I'll tell Mom you sent your regards."

"Yeah, tell her I'll come next time. For sure."

~~

Dev parked his black Porsche Turbo in the garage and walked to the mailbox by the street. He tucked the bottle of scotch under his arm and sorted through some bills as he entered his house through the front door, unlocked as usual. Living in a gated community near the racetrack, surrounded by a twenty-foot hedge, it wasn't the kind of neighborhood where anyone ever bothered.

"Hello," he yelled.

His voice echoed off the marble floor of the foyer. Leo, their Labrador retriever, was laying in the doorway to the den and barely raised his head. He left the bottle on the kitchen counter and went upstairs, where he heard the shower running.

"Need some company in there?" he said.

Yvonne opened the shower door, grabbed a white towel off a hook and started to dry herself. She made no effort at modesty as Dev made his way toward her, pulling off his shirt. He moved close and tried to kiss her neck.

"Not now, sweetie," she said. "I got a mani-pedi in twenty minutes, over in Glendale."

He noticed that she barely had any tan lines, but she did have a red patch on her neck that her straight blonde hair didn't quite cover. She began dressing, her only focus on the mirror as she pursed her lips, tossed her hair, and batted her eyelashes at her reflection.

"What happened there?" he said, lightly moving her hair.

She stepped away and slid into a short skirt that perfectly displayed her long legs. He watched as she pulled a pale blue cashmere sweater over her head. She didn't like to wear a bra. Angered, he grabbed her arm and pulled her close, gripping her by the throat.

"I asked you what happened to your neck."

"Nothing," she said, pushing him away. "God, you maniac. Cool it with the rough stuff. I'm not in the mood."

He put his shirt back on and sulked.

"I'm starving," he said. "Had to do one-sixteen today. Haven't had anything to eat since yesterday. Maybe some of those dumplings they got at Din Tai?"

"I can't," she said. "Rebecca's wedding is a week from Saturday, I have to fit in a size two. She's such a tiny little thing. I hate her. I left you a note. There's a veggie quiche in the fridge, or go on over to The Derby and get something at the bar. I just can't eat tonight."

She grabbed her purse.

"Later," she said. She waved her middle finger at him and was gone.

Dev found her note on the kitchen counter, propped up against a can of dog food. It was written on the back of a used envelope.

"Gone to get my nails done and then book club. Won't be too late – Y."

He found it annoying, the way she always doodled a smiley face on her notes, like she was a high school valley girl. He warmed the quiche in the microwave, added a side of cottage cheese and a handful of oyster crackers. Popping the top of a Corona Light, Dev settled in to watch a program on NOVA about seaweed and jellyfish that started him thinking that sushi would have tasted pretty good right now. He could feel the resentment rise at the reality of another evening alone when he was married to a perfectly healthy female who should be grateful for all manner of physical attention. Setting his plate aside, he kicked back the lounge chair and placed his hand on his chest. First finger, second, third, pinkie. He took a deep breath and slowly exhaled. The jellyfish floated.

After a minute had gone by, he kicked the chair upright.

"Fucking waste of time," said Dev, reaching for the *Racing Form.* "Should've gone to The Derby."

~~

Paula put her Starbucks cup on the roof of the car while she searched for her house keys. She needed a double Americano over ice to take the edge off after her yoga class, especially one like today when she'd spent most of the hour grinding her teeth between poses and holding her breath a lot more than she breathed in and out.

She made two trips to the kitchen with the groceries and then reached for the sugar on the top shelf to sweeten the coffee. Returning the sugar cannister, she bumped the old cookie tin where she kept her mad money. It was light. Her teeth went back to grinding.

I can't believe he broke into my piggy bank to bet on his stupid tip, she thought.

She went to her dresser and found her underwear drawer ajar, where she kept her emergency roll. *Jesus, the asshole has cleaned me out.*

Rube parked his ancient Jeep Wrangler in the last row of the free lot at Santa Anita. The track charged five bucks for the preferred lot which would have saved a hundred-yard hike, as if that mattered to him. *Five dollars at 20-to-1,* he thought, *that's another hundred bucks, just for walking two minutes.* He used a coupon from the newspaper for admission, paid the two-fifty for a program, and headed to the paddock.

Barry was leaning on the white railing around the walking ring, sporting a green celluloid visor like a bad version of a hustler in an all-night card game, with striped pants and a clashing checked shirt. It was a ridiculous look, but at the track he was just another maladjusted bachelor who grabbed the first thing he saw before heading out the door.

Contemplating Barry's wardrobe, Rube idly wondered about the truth of his friend's allegedly generous endowment. It must be true, Rube thought. He's too ugly otherwise. Why would all those women sleep with him if it wasn't true? Then again, the man could talk a monkey out of a tree.

"You sure this is a good idea?" said Rube.

"This, my boy, is a golden opportunity," said Barry, at which point he launched into a monologue detailing what a brilliant gambler he must be to avail himself and his friend with such exclusive inside information.

Rube pointed out that they are only here for one reason, and if he wanted to be inspired, he would try church on Sundays instead of his usual form of worship, which was the three-grand guaranteed Texas Hold'em game at Larry Flint's Hustler Casino over in Downey. And which, not for nothing, was a lot closer to home than Santa Anita, all the way across L.A.

"She said this is the race? Where is she?" said Rube.

"Over there," said Barry, motioning toward the saddling area. "She'll get the high-sign from him if it's a go. Wouldn't be a good idea for us to be seen together."

"Yeah, I guess," said Rube. "He sees you with her and gets the wrong idea, he might stiff the horse."

"He might be suspicious already," said Barry. "Almost caught us the other day."

"Shit," said Rube.

"I couldn't find the match cover she wrote her new cell number on, so I called her house and he answered."

"What happened when you called?"

"What do you think happened?" he answered. "I hung up."

"So you haven't talked to her?" Rube said. "How are we sure this is the right race?"

"Stop, will you? This is the right race," said Barry. "We met at that motel in Van Nuys last night and we worked things out, if you know what I mean."

He made a rude gesture that was hardly necessary to get the point across.

"How much money did you raise?" he said. "I got three hundred."

"I scratched together two-eighty," said Rube.

He wondered if Paula would notice the three double sawbucks and the fifty he borrowed from her stash.

"This horse better win," he said.

Less than half an hour later, Yvonne joined the group getting their photo taken in the winner's circle after Dev's horse broke like a shot and went on to win by five. She and one of the owner's daughters were the only ones under fifty, and no one but her was dressed in Chanel. Her pale-yellow suit matched the silks worn by her husband on the winning horse. The owner's wife couldn't take her eyes off Yvonne's three-carat diamond. That, and the Louboutin stilettos.

Barry nodded toward the odds board displaying a $20.40 win payoff.

"I guess she's not the only one he tells when he likes one," Barry said. "It sure wasn't our five-eighty that dropped it from 20-to-1 in that last flash."

"Better than losing," said Rube.

Even at 9-to-1, Rube figured he would still be taking home nearly three-grand, which was more folding money than he'd touched in months.

"You cash the tickets, I'll meet you later at my place," said Barry. "I gotta hook up with her at the Embassy Suites for a quickie while he's still riding."

Rube made a crack about everybody riding somebody, but Barry just walked away.

~~

"Barry says he wants to move here permanently when he gets his bonus," said Sally. "Going to get a place by the beach. He says we should move in together, that it'll be more affordable for me. Mainly to help me, he says, 'cause he doesn't need to."

"That's what they all say," said Paula. "Only here to help us."

"Like he likes that flea-trap he lives in," said Sally. "I always have to take a shower after I've been there."

Sally sat on the edge of the couch, finished her last swallow of wine, and reached for the bottle. She was trying to drop twenty pounds but losing the battle. She spent a few hundred last week at the Lulu Lemon shop, leaving there with what the girl told her was the latest in yoga wear. And very flattering, too, in the shade of aqua that looked great with her big green eyes, the girl had said.

"I don't know, he's been acting strange lately," said Sally. "Hope he's not cheating on me. Did he cheat on you?"

"I told you, we went out maybe twice about four years ago," said Paula. "It wasn't like we were dating. They're all strange, if you ask me."

"Barry lies all the time, but he's a bad liar," said Sally. "Told me he was taking me out to dinner last Sunday at the Palm and called me from the dock at five o'clock to say he just got in from fishing. Did I want fish for dinner? He'd clean it up and I could cook it? Shows up at nine with no fish and a snoot full."

"I guess I should be glad Rube's gambling and not doing another slut from the strand," said Paula. "We've been on a bad run lately, and now he thinks they're going to win big at the track. I'm about done with all of his bullshit, but I don't have enough money to move out. Guess I'm stuck for the time being."

"You can stay here with me and my sister," said Sally. "But I don't think the couch will suit you for long."

She topped off their glasses with the last of the wine.

"I'll be okay," said Paula. "I'll figure something out. Maybe these clowns will accidentally stumble on a winner and I'll get back what he's grabbed from my underwear drawer. Maybe they'll go hiking up Mount Wilson and fall off a cliff and we could collect on the insurance. That'd be enough to pay for a week at the Langham."

"Send him packing and tell him to take Barry with him," said Sally. "They can sit on a bench at the beach and smoke dope, or get real ambitious and write a screenplay nobody will ever read."

~~

Barry slicked back his hair, still damp from a shower, as Yvonne finished dressing in front of a full-length mirror. She saw him look in her direction and flashed him, pulling up her skirt to show she wasn't wearing anything underneath.

"He doesn't say anything when you show up late?" he said.

"He knows I won't sit there waiting for him like one of his little whores," she said. "And it gives him a little time to hit on the sluts at the bar."

Dev backed into his usual parking spot at Houston's on Arroyo Parkway and slipped the parking attendant a twenty. He pulled on a black Prada leather jacket and checked his reflection in the front door. Happy Hour participants were two-deep at the bar and a couple of blondes recognized him right away and made space.

"Usual, jock?" asked the bartender.

"And give my friends a refill," said Dev, winking at the girls.

"Yours is on me," said the bartender. "Had you in the feature."

"You're that jockey," said one of the girls, stifling a giggle.

Dev looked them over like he would the *Racing Form*, handicapping for the right angle. He took a sip of his cocktail.

"So," he said, "have you ladies ever heard what they say about jockeys?"

~~

Barry stacked the cash on the kitchen table in piles of one hundred dollars, all the bills facing the same way.

"A little OCD, are you?" said Rube.

"A little," said Barry. "That's how they do it at the bank."

"Some people count stairsteps, some have to put their clothes on the same way every time."

"Yeah, I count stairs sometimes," said Barry. "Vonnie says her old man says all the jockeys do that, like put on the same boot first, put the same leg first in their britches every time, stuff like that."

"Are you telling your old lady how much we won?" asked Rube.

Barry shot him a look, raised an eyebrow.

"Yeah, Sally, she might not be around much more," said Barry. "We weren't seeing stuff the same way. Thinks we should move in together, like that's gonna happen. This crazy one might be all I can handle anyway."

"Think I should tell Paula?" said Rube. "They talk, you know, yours and mine. Or hold back a few hundred for the next time?"

He wondered if he could get away with it, not telling her at all and just keeping the money. If the whole getting married thing wasn't going to work out anyway, maybe it was better to move out and keep the cash.

"Here," said Barry. "It's a good kind of problem."

He pushed a thick stack of bills at Rube.

~~

The dimly lit banquette was the last booth in the back room of the Arroyo Chop House, where they sat when they didn't want to be bothered.

Dev cut his steak into small bites. It was his way of stretching the meal, making it last. He didn't like doing what the jockeys called flipping, which was eating a big meal and then throwing it up. Dev tried flipping a few times but thought it wasn't worth beating up his GI tract. Also, it made your teeth look lousy, and he liked his teeth. He went to the dentist every two months and had them whitened, and always flashed a big smile in the winner's circle. Picking at small bites, he felt more like a normal person who didn't have to run four miles every morning and sit in the hot box to shed that last pound to make the weight for a big race. The occasional starvation did the trick.

"I have to stop at the store on the way home," Yvonne said. "Do you need anything?"

"What's with your neck?" he said. "It's still red."

She touched the spot that Barry's whiskers had burned.

"I think maybe it was the sweater I wore yesterday," she said. "Might be an allergy. I'm going to get some Benadryl. That'll fix it."

Dev popped the last piece of steak in his mouth and nodded, giving her the chance to change the subject.

"Is that other one you like still running tomorrow? In the last race?"

He nodded.

"Maybe we can hit the tri if we wheel her," he said. "Depends on what everybody else is doing. Wear that outfit again, maybe? Same owner."

"I can't wear the same thing twice, silly," she said. "I'll see you at home. You're going to the shrink again, right?"

He nodded, avoiding eye contact. She gave him a peck on the cheek and headed for the door.

~~

Paula stared at the cash, wondering how much Rube actually had won if this was just what he was showing her.

"Was this a one-time thing or what?" she said

"Hope not," said Rube. "Barry's still tight with the jockey's wife. She tells him when the jock's going to win at a price."

"Tight, huh?" she said.

She counted off the twenties and separated a handful.

"One-ten from the mad money jar and another eighty from my underwear drawer, plus ten for interest," she said and handed back the rest. "Money, but not exactly a huge pile of money."

He stared at the ceiling and waited for her next remark, which would be some crack about Barry's past performances.

"They better put another one over before she realizes he's a total lame-o," said Paula. "Or before her husband figures out she's doing some riding of her own."

"It's nothing like that," said Rube. "They're just friends."

The lie was so obvious she could only roll her eyes. Rube counted the remaining bankroll, which came to a little over two grand.

"At least we have enough for the rent," she said. "Go pay it first thing tomorrow so we don't have to duck old man Dooley all weekend."

She plucked a hundred-dollar bill from his hand.

"And I'll run over to Vons and pick up a couple of New York strips, baking potatoes, and a bottle of red."

"He says she probably has another one tomorrow that we can bet on," said Rube.

"Pay the rent first," said Paula.

~~

Sunday afternoon, and Barry and Rube were walking in from the free lot which was more than half full, a good turnout for a weekend card.

"This train might not run forever," said Barry. "She's as nuts as they come. Wanted me to tie her up and carry her up to the roof of the hotel yesterday and do it there in broad daylight. Said it turns her on."

"Hard to believe her old man's still not wise," said Rube.

"Of the two of them, he's the one who delivers, and this is our big chance," said Barry. "The last race is a trifecta with a full field, twelve horses. We get lucky and a couple of longshots finish second and third, we might make a real score."

"I dunno," said Rube. "Hate to blow a chance when the favorite runs in and the tri comes back paying nothing. Just saying."

"So we bet to win, mostly, and wheel the tri," said Barry. "Cover ourselves."

They were getting close to the grandstand gate when Yvonne's Jaguar suddenly appeared, peeling out of the jockeys' lot and hitting the curb as it turned toward the Baldwin Avenue exit.

"What the hell's going on?" said Rube.

"Apparently nothing," said Barry. "She took off like the cops were chasing her. I guess the bet's off for today."

His cell phone beeped with a text.

"It's her," he said. "I gotta go."

Rube didn't hear a peep from Barry the rest of that day and well into Monday morning. He put in a few hours at work, then spent a lunch "hour" at the Venice pier with some of his doper pals who were still intent on solving the world's problems. By the time he drove home he never expected to find a parking spot right in front of their place. Neither was he expecting to see Barry sitting on the stoop.

"Big problem, pal," said Barry.

Whenever Barry was in a jam, or needed money, or found himself in a dicey situation with a woman, he wouldn't make eye contact. And he wasn't making eye contact now, which led Rube suspect any combination of all three.

"Let me guess," Rube said, only halfway serious. "She wants to leave her husband for lover boy Barry."

"It's no joke," Barry said. "Says she's leaving him and packing up to move in with me. I told her she's crazy."

"She knows you live in a shoebox, right?" said Rube. "And that you already have a girlfriend?"

Barry was looking somewhere off in space.

"I told her I live in a condo by the ocean in Santa Monica and write screenplays," he said. "I told her I just sell luxury cars to supplement my income until I get my Netflix deal wrapped up. Without me asking, she says the jockey has a gun, the same one he threatened another jockey with one time, just for talking to her. He knocks her around plenty too. I'm not getting shot for any psycho broad."

"Condo by the ocean, huh," said Rube.

"I didn't want her to think I'm a loser."

"She would have figured that out eventually."

"Hey, I don't need you to bust my balls," said Barry. "Anyway, she said he already knows. Said she told him there was someone else, and he went postal. She thinks he checked her phone and found all the texts and now he wants to kill me."

Barry rubbed his face and looked at his hands.

"I gotta leave town," he said. "Can you front me a grand?"

"You had the same amount as me, from the score," said Rube. "I just paid the rent. Where's yours?"

"Lost it at Commerce last night. Playing Pai Gow."

"Shit," said Rube.

"I was ahead almost three thousand."

"Idiot."

"Here," said Barry, holding out his car keys. "Take me to the airport. I gotta blow."

"You kidding?" said Rube.

Paula walked out onto the porch just as Barry's phone beeped an incoming text. His face flushed as he read the message.

"C'mon guys, get in the car," he said. "It's life and death."

~~

Dev was lying face down in a pool of crimson on the kitchen floor. A trickle of blood ran down the side of his head. There was a chrome plated .38 on the floor next to him. The left side of Yvonne's face and her eye was puffy and she was disheveled to the extent Rube wasn't sure he recognized her from the track.

"Jesus," said Rube.

"Jesus," said Paula. "Is he dead?"

"He smacked me and started poking me all over with that gun, so I whacked him with the blender," she said. "Put it in my mouth, then in my crotch, like he was going to stick it in me, the prick."

"Jesus," said Barry. "That's a lot of blood."

"Dragon fruit," said Yvonne. "It looks just like blood. I was making a smoothie."

Yvonne touched her face. She had a carving knife in her other hand.

"Here, honey," said Paula. She took the knife away and put it in a drawer.

"I was thinking of cutting his dick off, but I guess that wouldn't be self-defense," said Yvonne, laughing as she pushed the pistol toward Barry with her foot. "Shoot him for me. We can say I did it when he beat me."

Barry backed up a little.

"Shoot him?"

"He'll kill me for sure when he wakes up. Kill us both. Just do it. We can bury him in the yard. He was beating me."

"Maybe we should call the police," said Rube.

"Yeah, we should call the police," said Paula.

"They never do anything," said Yvonne. "They been here a dozen times. He tells them he'll give them a winner and they never do anything. Mister big-shot jockey."

She aimed a kick at Dev's ribs but slipped and landed in the dragon fruit juice spreading around him.

"Shit," she said, looking at her stained blouse. "I just bought this top."

Barry pulled Rube and Paula aside as Yvonne sat crying on the floor.

"She's nuts," said Rube.

"I told you so," said Barry.

"You're both fucking idiots," said Paula as she dialed 9-1-1. "Somebody get a mop."

www.ingramcontent.com/pod-product-compliance
Lightning Source LLC
Chambersburg PA
CBHW070924130626
46555CB00001B/276